Motivation Part II:
The Chase

by

Swift

R H Publishing, LLC
P.O.Box11642
Milwaukee, WI 53211

R H Publishing, P.O. Box 11642, Milwaukee, WI 53211
or email us at: talk2us@rhpublishings.com .
Visit our website @ www.swiftnovels.com

First Printing: July 2013
10 9 8 7 6 5 4 3 2 1
ISBN-13: 978-0615834658
1. Urban 2. Fiction
Printed in the United States of America
Cover designed by Devise Printing

Dedicated to: my brother Lil Marv
a.k.a. Six Million

Gone, but your memory
will forever live on . . .

Foreword

When my big bro Swift called and asked me to write a foreword in his upcoming book on my dear friend Marvin I felt honored. I also knew that it would be a daunting task because I had so many memories of Lil Marv and I really did not know where to start. After careful thought, I decided to go with my heart and write about the impact that he had on my life.

I met Lil Marv in the summer of 1990 through some mutual friends out of our hood. I was 12 years old and he was 16 years old. We did a move that same day and I recall that the only thing that he was concerned about was keeping this red remote control car so that he can take it home to his little brother. From that day forward, we built a bond that was inseparable. I remember hanging out the whole summer of 1990 until he caught a case that got him sent to Ethan Allen School (Wales). We continued to hangout throughout our teenage years whenever either of us was not doing time in Wales.

As we grew into men, our bond became stronger. Marvin was always like a big brother to me. When we ran the streets, together he would criticize the things that I did wrong and he gave me the proper knowledge to tighten up my game. Sometimes I think back when I first entered the game and decided to diversify my street portfolio. I tried my hand in pimping for the first time it was Lil Marv that was there every step of the way to show me the ropes. He never turned down the opportunity to hit the highway with me even when at times he did not have a hoe to take with him. He always kept me entertained and there was never a dull moment.

Lil Marv had a unique character that I do not think I can fully explain within this concise writing. But, what I will say is that he had the special ability and charm to breathe life into any room. He was naturally funny and always knew what to say to make people laugh. Those that really knew Marv understand the special quality that I speak of. To this day I reminisce about some of the things he have said and done and it makes me chuckle. He was truly the life of the party.

My fondest memory of Marvin Thomas is when he accepted Islam and I began to see his life take a drastic change. It was as if he started to live with meaning because of his fear of Allah. So we were not only bonded by the streets, but we were also bonded by our spirituality. It always brought joy to him when I could make it to Jumuah to pray with him on Friday. I can recall him calling my phone in search of Islamic knowledge. He would enjoy listening to me recite Surat out of the Qur'an in Arabic. November 15, 2011 was no different Lil Marv called and asked me when was the next time I would be going to the mosque to pray. I did not know that it would be the last conversation we would have. He was tragically murdered just hours later.

I would like to end this foreword with an Ayat (verse) from the Qur'an: Every soul shall have a taste of death: And only on the Day of Judgment shall you be paid your full recompense. Only he who is saved far from the Fire and admitted to the Garden will have attained the object (of Life): For the life of this world is but goods and chattels of deception. (3: 185)

Salaam, Dank

Motivation Part II: The Chase

Chapter One

The afternoon sun beamed heavily upon them as they picnicked in Michelle Watson's backyard. Summer had yet to come, but the temperature had reached 81 degrees by 1:00 pm and with hardly any wind or shade, it made the early June weather feel closer to 100 degrees. Michelle and Keysha decided on the gathering for Key and Brandon. Brandon was due to be sentenced on his weed charge conviction. He'd taken a deal for two years and only had a few days of freedom before he had to turn himself in.

Michelle hadn't had the opportunity to sit and chat with her son in quite some time after what she'd heard about Red's murder she began to worry more about his well-being; knowing that he was involved in things that were bringing about people dying, not to mention Key being shot himself. Now, all of a sudden she started to regret her acceptance of countless gifts that he had showered upon her via his destructive livelihood and manipulative ways. When Key arrived back in Milwaukee everything took a turn for the better with her and Keysha so fast that she neglected to see the dangers that came along with what he did for a living. But today Michelle assured herself that she's make an effort to encourage him to put an end to it all.

When Key arrived, he parked in the back on a concrete slab next to his mothers' garage, extra cautious of his surroundings after the ambush on him and Red that fateful night. And the last thing he wanted was to bring that element of violence to his family's home. Keysha was the first to greet him as he submerged through the wooden security gate separating the yard from the alley.

"Hey bro!" she said running over to embrace him.

"What's going on here? I thought y'all were just throwing a few things on the grill, who are all these people?" Key said scanning the crowd.

"They're just some of our friends. How's your arm dude and why haven't you called us?" she said in a concerned sisterly tone.

"I'm alright sis, I just didn't wanna worry ma' you know."

"Well you need to step back from all that stuff bro. I can't believe they killed Red," she said with tears filling hers eyes, "Do you know who did it?"

Come on introduce me to your friends was all Key said as he wrapped his arm around her shoulder. Key had enough on his mind and he would rather forget about it all for now. After the chat with Kimmie at the hospital, he could use a few laughs to take his mind off all the questions that lingered in regards to his freedom. Discovering that one of your top hos was actually not a ho at all, but a special agent for the

F.B.I. was enough to make the iciest of pimps run for the hills.

After meeting Keysha's friends and exchanging pleasantries with the other guest, he headed into the house to find his mother.

Michelle was in the kitchen with their aunt Hazel preparing some side dishes to go along with the meat they were grilling out back.

"Hey ma..."

She turned around displaying a warm smile as they both embraced.

"You look tired baby," she said wiping her lipstick off his cheek, "You had been sleeping right?"

"Yeah ma," he said before saying hello to his aunt.

"Hey baby," Hazel said as they hugged before she proceeded outside to check the grill.

"I spoke with Devin's mother the other day; she's devastated by that boys' death. I feel so sorry for them," she said shaking her head. "How you been doing Keyshawn? I know that was your best friend and..."

"Can we please not talk about it right now ma?" He knew that she would go on and on about it had he not said anything to stop her. It hadn't even been a full week and the funeral was still to come. There would be plenty of time to talk about, but today was not the day because the pain was still too fresh.

"Okay," she said patting him on his hand, "But what you gonna do with yourself now Keyshawn?"

"What you mean ma?"

"You know what I mean; it's time for you to step away from all that baby. I don't won't anything happening to you Lord knows I couldn't stand it if I had to bury one of my babies."

"I'm alright ma. You don't have to worry."

"No you're not alright boy! Now I may not have been in the streets but I'm not naive to them either." Keyshawn dropped his head. "Look baby, all I'm saying is that you really need to start doing something else with yourself now. That club y'all opened, now that was a good idea, and I have a friend who owns a mortgage company. She can help you make some productive moves with your money. And while you're at it enrolling in school don't sound like such a bad idea either."

"School?"

"Yes school. You said that like it's a disease or something. Ain't nothing wrong with you furthering your education now baby, you should consider it."

"I don't know ma', I'll talk to your friend but I'm not sure about that school stuff," he said thinking that it would satisfy her, hoping the subject would change. He wasn't sure if he'd be on the streets to see next month. So plans were secondary at this point he wanted to share everything with his mom, but elected not to knowing, that it would only add on more stress.

"Okay, we'll go see her sometime next week. But I still want you to think school over. And you need to move..."

"Ma, I am moving, I'll be doing that real soon."

"But you don't need to be staying at that place. What if those people come back over there?"

"They're not Ma,'" he said trying to downplay her concern.

"How do you know that Keyshawn, I have the mind to ask you what happened for them to come to your house with that, but I think I really don't wanna know. Now here's a key to..."

"Ma, I'm okay, I don't need to move in with you," he said with a confident smile.

Michelle wasn't convinced; she sat the keys on the counter-top. "Just in case you change your mind or need to use them. You and your sister are all I've got I just don't know what I'd do" she began to cry.

"I'll take the keys ma' okay, here wipe your face," he said handing her a napkin off the table.   "Come on let's join the picnic, people outside having fun and you in here crying." He kissed her on the cheek, "Come on Ma."

~ ❖ ~

When Special Agent Greg Daley made it back to the F.B.I.'s field office, his partner Li Chan was leaving; their superior, Sidney Bender's office.

"What's up agent?" she said to Daley in a cheery mood.

"Nothing much, thought you stepped out?"

"I did, I just ran by my mother's she needed me to help her reorganize some furniture."

"Oh, well aren't you a wonderful daughter."

"Yeah, but seriously I've just been informed by Bender that we need to have this thing wrapped up by next week."

"Really, what's the rush all of a sudden?" Daley said with a curious look.

"I think he's getting pressure from Madison, but of course he didn't confirm that with me. Anyway, I just thought I'd let you know. Are you going to be in for the rest of the afternoon?"

"Yeah, why?"

"I wanted to go over a few things about that Smith guy. You know kinda familiarize myself with that aspect of the investigation." Daley thought this was odd since her assigned target was Key and not T.A. But he played a fool to catch one, just as he did with the lie she'd told him about being at her mothers' place. Chan's strange behavior towards the end of her undercover work was the match that ignited Daley to wonder if she'd gotten herself into more than just an undercover operation with Keyshawn. He knew that sometimes agents would go too far undercover and engage in things that could confuse their interest in the subjects they were after. So when she left the office earlier he tracked the bureau's vehicle through GPS to the hospital to see if his suspicions held any weight. Now with what he found along with her lying, he was certain that something inappropriate and unethical had to be going on.

"Okay, give me an hour and we can hook-up in my office. I have his file down there, was there anything in particular that you wanted to know?"

Yes, I'd like to know how I can make that whole file disappear without anyone noticing, she said to herself before answering. "No just a general overview of what we have will be fine."

When she left, Chan went down to a friend in the "Missing Children's" Unit. Seth Bennis, an expert in lost child investigations, used a cubicle as office, which was located in the rear of the division unit on the fourth floor.

"Hey buddy," she said peeking around the cubicle Seth was hard at work as usual.

"Ah, hello Li, what brings you down here, I thought you were busy busting pimps undercover," he said turning to face her.

"I am. I came down here because I need your help."

"Really, how may I be of assistance?"

"Well, I'm trying to find out if there's any connection between one of my subjects and the escorting of a minor..." She gave him the name of a girl that she knew had been missing along with an assortment of addition information that she'd manufactured herself.

Chan knew was Seth would be more than willing to stop whatever he was doing to help her. He had an office crush on the agent since forever. Something that she'd discovered when they worked an abduction case together in her early days at the bureau. But Seth was a geeky type of guy who lacked the confidence to do anything about his desires. Although Chan wouldn't have gone out with him if he'd asked her, she still made sure she was always nice to the poor sap. That's why she felt a little uneasy with regards to what she was about to do to him. Initially Chan had opted not to go through with the deceptive plan she'd devised. But after brainstorming the possibilities she derived to the conclusion that his job wouldn't be in any jeopardy, and pressed forward, taking full advantage of the easy mark.

As he navigated his way through various networks and databases in search of a ghost, Chan stalked each finger and keystroke patiently waiting for the naïve agent to reveal his password. She lured him into frivolous talk as he worked, skillfully playing above suspicion, and being sure to make immediate eye contact with him when his eyes drew away from the prompter. Once Seth was done with the wild goose chase she'd sent him on, Chan thanked him for his efforts and said her good-byes.

On the way to the elevators remembering (HARVARD) the password wasn't the problem, her issue was figuring the how and where she would breach the system without being discovered. But on the way up the elevator the answer dawned upon her as easily as she'd thought of it.

Chapter Two

When he rung Michelle's doorbell; Keysha was coming out of the bathroom downstairs.

"Ma, you want me to get it for you?" She yelled into the kitchen.

"No baby you can go out back I got it," she said wiping her hands with a towel. Michelle knew who was at the door and didn't want to ruin the surprise.

After Keysha went out back, she answered the door. He was standing at the threshold wearing a pleasant but nervous smile. A splitting image of the twins; with the same stature as Keyshawn; had he asked for a DNA test the judge would have surely held him in contempt for insulting his intelligence.

"Hello Tim," Michelle said as she stepped aside to allow him entry.

"Hello Michelle."

"I wasn't sure if you were coming, but I'm glad you did. They are gonna be so happy to see you Tim. You can go in the kitchen," she said closing the door.

"This is a nice place you have here Chelle," he said looking around in approval. Hearing him call her that brought back memories from distant years when they were back in McComb. Tim was the only person who called her "Chelle." Everybody else back home referred to her as "Tweet," a name given by her father when she was a little girl.

"Thanks, would you like something to drink?"

"Yeah, sure," he said standing near the kitchen table.

Just then, Keysha came strolling through the back door. Caught completely off guard she couldn't believe what she was seeing.

"Daddy, what you doing here," She asked on her way over to hug him.

"Hey Kesh, I came by to see y'all. Your mother invited me over," he said glancing at Michelle, who was near tears. All she ever wanted was for him to be a part of her kids' lives and for Tim to see one day how much they loved and needed him around.

"Oh, so this was your surprise huh ma'?" Keysha said looking at Michelle.

She didn't respond.

"Where's your brother at baby?" Tim said feeling a little bit at ease after having had such a warm welcome from his daughter, one that he wasn't so sure of until now. It had been years since she's seen him yet was still able to show him genuine love. Love that he's neglected for most of her life. He suddenly felt like a complete scumbag.

"He's outside, come on there's some people I'd like you to meet," she said pulling his arm. A proud daughter she was. Throughout the years, Keysha had never really written her father totally out of her life. She'd always hoped that one day they could have a real relationship.

As they were on their way out Aunt Hazel was coming in to get eating utensils for the guests. She looked at Tim without saying a word as they passed one another. Hazel; along with everyone else in the family; despised Tim for the way he'd done his children. She pitched in to help Michelle with the kids all those years that her niece struggled. So she'd seen; first hand; all the pain and broken promises Tim had brought upon them, and for that she could find no respect for him. To her he was less than a man, a coward and was never deserving of her niece to begin with. Tim saw the look that she'd given him and he understood her position. He was just hoping that his son didn't feel the same as she did.

Keyshawn was mackin' at Keysha's friend Nydia when his father appeared walking through the yard with Keysha holding his hand. His attitude instantly turned icy. Nydia noticed him looking over her shoulder, as he grew quiet; the mask he now wore prompted her to look back.

"Is everything alright? Who's that?" she said.

"Nobody important," She knew something wasn't right and when they came closer she quickly noticed the resemblance.

"Here is my daddy girl, Daddy this is my friend Nydia." They exchanged pleasantries before he focused his attention on Key.

"What's up son? You don't recognize your old man?" Tim said with a nervous laugh.

"What you doing here? And don't come calling me yo' fuckin' son!" he said with a murderous stare. Keysha lead Nydia away, attempting to prevent her from hearing the oncoming conflict.

"Look, I'm sorry; I know I haven't been much of anything to you. I understand your anger and whatever resentment you might have for me Keyshawn. I'm sure if I were you I'd feel the same way. Key stared at him for a while unable to speak. All the many nasty things that he planned on telling his father once he saw him again were still very fresh in his mind. But due to the rearing of his mother, aunt, and grandmother he couldn't bring himself to do it. As a kid "respect your parents" and "keep family business in the family" was instilled in him as a virtue of life. With all this flashing in his mind Keyshawn simply got up and moved from the area.

All the guests were watching in amazement but Keysha did her best to bring the atmosphere normal. She escorted Tim over to meet Brandon.

Back in the house, Keyshawn was heated by the surprise of Tim's arrival as he spoke with Michelle in regards to the situation.

"Mama why you ain't tell me dude was coming?"

"I didn't tell you because I knew you'd make a big deal of it and not want to come if he was here. Besides your father...."

"Ma, please don't call that nigga my father, I told you I don't have one of those."

"Boy first of all don't, ever cut me off while I'm speaking and what I tell you about using that word in my presence. You hear me Keyshawn?" she stared at him with that, "I'll kick yo' ass look."

"Yeah ma' I hear you." Despite what he did in the streets, his mother was queen.

"I ain't Tim you talk to me like you got some sense."

"Ma', all I'm saying is you coulda' told me he was coming."

"I know, but I didn't! Now I apologize for that but you have to move past all that hostility. How many times I gotta' tell you that baby?" Michelle had always been a forgiving person; she tried her best to pass on that trait onto them. Keysha was an easy sell on this one out of a daughters love and desperation to have her father. But Keyshawn was viewing the situation from a man's eyes and he couldn't see past the cowardice of it all.

"I just don't see how you can be so willing to forgive the dude. I mean after all that you've been through ma 'he didn't even try to help ma'." Michelle looked in his eyes seeing the hurt, anger, and disgust but could think of no other words to say. "I'm sorry, but I'm not just willing to forget that easy. He ain't cared in all these years, so why should I now? Cause he's over here, over here at a time when we don't need him no more. Now, you can forgive him ma' but I say he can go back to Detroit or wherever he just came from, he's dead to me! I gotta' make a run I'll be back in a minute."

"You can't blame him for feeling that way baby. He's not wrong," Hazel, said walking into the kitchen. She heard them talking from down the hall but didn't want to interfere.

"I know auntie I know" she wanted to be mad at Tim for bringing their son to hate him so much, but pity and sympathy for him overshadowed it. Tim had called two weeks ago telling her that he'd been diagnosed with throat cancer and it had become terminal. The doctors were giving him four months to live and he wanted to at least make amends with his children before he died. She knew that deep down Key had a profound love for his father, he was just disappointed in him, and this was his way of expressing it.

Key phoned T.A. when he left they agreed to meet up at the club. When he arrived, T.A. had three young gorillas outside all armed and ready for trouble. Inside he found two more soldiers playing pool with their weapons displayed on top of the bar. Proceeding through the fortress, he eventually located T.A.in the Platinum room orientating two white chicks who were new to his stable. T.A. excused himself and the two went into the office where they could talk in private.

"I see security's tight around here homie," he said pouring himself a heavy glass of Louis XIII. Keyshawn wasn't a drinker and certainly not at four in the afternoon. T.A. was watching in confusion and wondered if it was all just the bullets flying that had his friend outside of himself.

"Yeah man, I'm not taking any chances. I just wish we could have thought to have some folks with y'all that night. Pour me up some of that will you." Key handed him the cognac and he took a sip.

"I can't believe my nigga gone T."

"I know homie, but that shit ain't over I'm gonna make those fags pay for pulling that stunt. I've been doing my homework and I'm pretty sure I know where one of them stay. I've had people staked outside the punks' house but he hasn't been there in a few days."

"Which one is it?"

"Fox, I paid a few thousand for the info and from what I hear they all can be found there if we catch them on the right day. So don't even worry about it, I'm aiming to have these dudes faded all at once."

"That's good fam, but we got bigger problems on our hands." T.A. put his drink down.

"Now what is it?" he said not having the slightest clue, but all of a sudden became nervous as hell.

"You remember when I told you I smelled something fishy with that bitch Kimmie?"

"Yeah, I thought you cleared all that up though?"

"So did I, but it turns out I was right all along."

"You was right about what, the bitch being the police?" Key shook his head yes. T.A. busted out in laughter.

"Man get the hell outta' here. Real funny, good one!" he said picking up his drink.

"I wish I was playing, but I'm dead serious pimp. I just got the whole scoop from the broad earlier this afternoon."

"Wait a minute, you telling me that this chick is an undercover fed, and she told you? That shit don't sound right, you sure she wasn't just trying to get out a nigga grips?"

"Listen man, I'm one hundred percent sure the bitch know everything. They running a full-scale investigation on us right now player, and they're planning on having indictments real soon."

"What? So when you say us you mean me and you?"

"Yeah, it was actually me, you, and Red. Apparently this shit has been going on ever since I met the bitch man."

"I can't believe this Key. And I thought you said that you fucked the bitch?"

"I did, and get this, the bitch is pregnant!"

"Okay pimp that's enough, you got my attention now let's take this whole thing from the top. I need to hear this shit blow by blow." They both sat down as Key began telling him all that he knew over a game of chess.

Chapter Three

Special Agent Li Chan and Greg Daley were both in his office going over the file on T.A. when she suddenly began to feel sick.

"Excuse me agent, I have to use the restroom" Chan said hastily rising from her seat and out the door.

When she left the room, he waited about a minute before going for the leather briefcase that she'd left sitting in the chair. Moving swiftly he rummaged through the bags contents in search of anything that would reveal what she had going on under the surface with Keyshawn Watson. Inside the main area, there was nothing but a few files and some procedural forms that were required during investigations. But on the outside of the case he felt a small lump in a pocket on the back of the bag. When he unzipped it, he was shocked to find a pamphlet labeled "Dealing with Morning Sickness" along with a bottle of pre-natal pills. He closed the case and placed it back in the seat. Within seconds, she was opening the door.

"Sorry about that Greg."

"It's not a problem, there wasn't much more to cover anyway. You know everything that I have on the case."

"Okay, well I better get going then. I still have a ton of paperwork to do before I go home and I sure don't wish to take it with me."

"I know what you mean. I'll call you if I need anything before you leave."

"Sure thing" she said before grabbing the briefcase and hitting the door. Daley was sure now that the vomiting in the conference room the other day and the frequenting of the lavatory could be explained by her pregnancy. But it just seemed odd to him seeing as though she never even mentioned having a significant other.

~ ~

They were into the third game of chess with Key winning the first two and a few moves away from another victory as well. T.A. had been performing terribly, so Key really didn't accredit the wins to his skills. He was pretty sure that the news he'd just laid on T.A. had occupied the better portion of his thinking process. They went over every possible outcome that could transpire following the feds case. And it was obvious that the best ones entailed Li Chan; as they now knew her; getting rid of the wire-taps somehow. An idea that T.A. wasn't too enthusiastic about, because as of now he couldn't actually foresee her pulling it off. The danger in a task of this magnitude was clear to him and he wasn't so sure that Chan would carry out her duties if given too much time to ponder it all.

"You gotta make sure you stay on top of that chick Key," he said partially focused on the game.

"Fasho' you ain't gotta tell me that. We both got a second phone to communicate when she gets off work. The other day she was talking about our future together with this kid=" T.A. cut him off.

"Make sure you nurture all that shit."

"No doubt, shit I've been thinking about flying to Vegas to marry this bitch. Don't they have a law preventing a wife from testifying on the husband against her will?"

"Yeah, and that's not a bad idea. Of course if she gets that blatant with it they gonna have a slew of charges to hit her ass with anyway so it won't matter."

"Better her than me player."

"I hear you, but let's hope it don't get that far huh. It's your move nigga."

"Check" Key said moving his queen next to T.A.'s king.

"That's checkmate. Damn you kicked my ass today."

"Man you weren't even into the game."

"I know. Dig, you remember that scheme we had going with the plastic? Have you thought about maybe pressing this chick to secure us that information we were missing" T.A. said with a slight grin.

His mention of "the plastic" snatched Key's attention. A few months back they gained access to some American Express Black Card accounts. Reserved exclusively for the wealthiest and privileged citizens of the world; these cards usually didn't come with small limits. So in essence, the cardholder could charge anything from a Bentley to a Gulf Stream G4 jet. They mainly purchased trinkets from personal jewelers of theirs in Milwaukee and Chicago that could easily be sold for tens of thousands of dollars. At times, they were able to secure cash advances; however, there was usually a limit of twenty-five thousand per transaction. The company allowed two transactions of this capacity before the user was required to verify certain personal information about the true cardholders' identity, thus then making the card worthless at which time they would destroy them. Together they netted over a quarter of a million dollars in less than sixty days off four cards they managed to obtain. A figure that could have easily ran into seven digits had they been able to just answer those simple questions. The thought of bringing in over a million bucks was one that Key could not resist.

"Now you got ya' thinking cap on T. what happened when you was playing chess?" He said jokingly.

"No paper was involved." They both started laughing. "Seriously though, I know we agreed to let that shit cool off. But the stakes are much greater my nigga. And let's assume this plan we have going with this fed bitch flops and she can't get us out of this shit. Well at least we'll have plenty bread to bury until we come home." T.A. said shrugging his shoulders.

"I feel you mane," Key said in agreement.

Later on that night Key, meet Chan at a restaurant in Fox Point which was a small suburban village on the outskirts of Milwaukee. Approximately twenty minutes outside the city, the place was an Italian eatery in a quiet area. Chan had gone there many times as a child with her parents

Her mood went from tired and weary to blissful and enthusiastic when Key walked through the door. But still a bit nervous; she could not keep from looking out the window in search of any suspicious vehicles that may have followed him.

"You made sure you didn't have a tail right?" She said in a low-tone.

"Yeah, of course," he said taking his seat. She'd chosen a booth in the rear of the restaurant because it provided a clear view of the entire area.

"Good, it's great seeing you. I know we just saw each other earlier but that seemed so much like business. I've got a million things I want to say to you. Things that I've been thinking about, you know like the baby, what we do next, and things like that." Key was inattentive and sort of glaring out the window in a thought that was nowhere near their table. "Baby, baby are you here with me?" Chan said breaking his trace.

"Oh yeah, yeah excuse me I was thinking about some shit with my father. He just came in town today and I ain't seen the dude in a decade." His lies were always superb, what he really had on his mind was those figures him and T.A. had contemplated.

"Wow that long huh. I couldn't imagine I'm sorry you probably don't want to talk about that."

"It's ok, so how was your day?" His performance continued.

"It was pretty good actually. Besides throwing up, a few times I would say it went well. I came a little closer to executing that plan we spoke about earlier as well," she said taking a sip of water. That was music to his ears; half of what he had come for was accomplished now it was time to see where her heart really was.

"Wonderful, you know baby I've been doing a little thinking about our future after all of this." Her face beamed off the sentence. Key knew he struck her in the heart dead center; telling her, precisely what she desired to hear at the moment. Not done yet, he leaned in gently placing both her hands in his and looked her directly in the eyes as he began to spit additional fire. "Baby I don't know how this is about to turn out but I do know one thing. I want you and my child in my life. I want to not only be there, but I wanna be a good father to him. I say him because I hope it's a boy." They both smiled, only his was manufactured. Key didn't give a shit about her or the baby she carried, as far as he was concerned they both could kick rocks and die. Just long as it transpired after she'd fulfilled her purpose. The game didn't stop simply because she was pregnant and into her feeli.ngs all of a sudden. In fact, that was only a signal for him to mash even harder. As a pimp, he cursed himself for making such a reckless mistake. But was pleased to be in a situation where he could rectify and capitalize off of it at the same time.

He continued with his concert. "I've always said that if I found myself in this situation that I would own up to my responsibilities as a man." He reached in his pocket and pulled out the small black box.

Completely overwhelmed, she began to tear up. It was as if he'd just read her heart and mind in answering her prayers. Clicking the box open, the diamond shined on her face like the sun after ten days of stormy rain. He got up and sat on the left side of her.

"You don't have to say a word yes I will marry you." She said wrapping her arms around him and planting a passionate kiss on his lips.

When the guest left the picnic, they sat in Michelle's living room and enjoyed quality-time alone getting caught-up on things they'd missed in each other's lives over the past years. Keysha was elated to learn that they had a younger brother and sister in Detroit. She always wanted a little sister, while staring at the pictures of them both she wondered what they were like and suddenly the anxiousness to meet them grew even stronger.

Keysha was crushed when Tim told her the news about is condition, yet she remained optimistic. "So what are the doctors saying? They can help you right?"

"That's one of the reasons I came to see you baby. It is not looking good they say I don't have much time. Since the cancer has spread to several organs within my body they really can't say at this point." He didn't want to tell her exactly how long just yet. Tim thought that would have been too much to lie on his baby girl all at once. He figured as his health worsened she'd gradually learn to accept losing him and by the time he was gone maybe would have come to terms with it all.

Keysha saw his broken spirits that was something she couldn't help but to sympathize with. "I'm so sorry daddy," she said getting up to hug him. Each time she'd called him daddy that day it gave him strength to clutch on to his life even more. Tim felt as though he didn't deserve the loyalty, respect, and understanding that she'd extended his way. He only wished his son felt the same.

"It's okay baby, and hey who knows, I might beat this. God has the final say on who lives and who dies right," he said wiping tears from her face. Keysha didn't say a word; emotions had gotten the best of her.

"I just want you to know that I love you baby and I'm sorry for not being a father to you doll. I missed so much and if I could turn back the clock, I would. There are so many things that I regret, but really being a part of you and your brothers' lives that has to be deepest. It's like a wound that won't heal." His voice began to crack. "Maybe I'm getting my just desserts"

"No you're not, daddy please don't say that. Let's just pray God has another outcome other than what the doctors are seeing."

"And if he doesn't?"

"We'll just have to make the best of what time we have left then won't we," she said in an effort to brighten the moment.

~ ~

They secured a room at a hotel near-by after finishing their meals. Key had yet to put the icing on the cake, but figured everything should be in place by the end of the night. They sat in the Jacuzzi while sipping on champagne. With one arm draped over her shoulders, she leaned into his chest as they watched the moon hang over the lake as it illuminated the room.

Key began by asking questions about what really went on behind the scenes at the FBI. As she spilled her guts revealing things he should not know, he suddenly felt a strong surge of supremacy almost as if he was indestructible. Li informed him about the new unit that had been assembled within the bureau to specifically target pimps; mainly the high profile types whom the government already had intelligence on. Dubbed the "Innocence and Trafficking Unit," their top priority was tracking down pimps who dealt in solicitation of minors across interstate lines.

Milwaukee along with nineteen other cities including Cleveland, Chicago, Miami, Phoenix, Detroit, New York, D.C., Atlanta, Dallas, and a slew of cities in Nevada and California were all placed on what the bureau called a "Blue List." Which meant that those cities would be the first spots this new unit would be implemented in with combined data and intel from offices throughout the nation; it was determined by the agency's best analyst that serious crimes committed by prostitutes who acted on the commands of a pimp were most prevalent in those areas. They also concluded that juveniles had committed over sixty percent of the offenses. Officials in the nations' capital had been concerned with a recent flow of video's and documentaries that were being produced by various pimps and production companies, many of which had originated from the Mid-West and Western states. Pimps were shown boasting about their extravagant lifestyles while displaying luxurious possessions they'd acquired by way of the illicit trade. Their women accompanied many of them, some of which law enforcement had found to be underage teens. That along with their blatant disregard for the law was two of the main reasons that compelled officials to devote more of the bureau's effort and resources into investigating and apprehending these types of individuals.

Months prior, Key and Red had been approached by a company in Chicago offering what they called a

'Consultant Fee' if they'd agreed to appear in a film and share their experience and knowledge of the life. Being young and adventurous they toyed with the idea. But acting on the advice of T.A., in the end they declined, and after hearing what Li just told him he was certain they'd made the correct choice. Here was proof of how foolish doing such a thing really was.

They went out on the balcony the breeze from Lake Michigan was soothing after an hour in the hot tub. After a few glasses of DP Key was feeling himself and felt on top of the world, ready to turn the heat all the way up now. "I have a picture in my mind of how I want things to be after all this Kimmie. And it doesn't involve any of this shit that's going on in my life now." He'd gotten use to calling her by the alias and it seemed unnatural calling her anything else. Li didn't mind it actually heightened the adventure.

"So tell me about it baby, what do you see?" She said smiling at him.

"Another life far away from here, but before we do that I want to take my chance at walking away with a million dollars. If I can pull it off we'll never look back baby."

"That's sounds good," she said.

"I know but I have to tell you in order for it to work I'm gonna need your help."

"You know that's not a problem just tell me what I need to do?"

"I need you to get some information about some people."

"Okay, tell me everything and I'll tell you what all can be done on my end."

He explained what the scheme entailed, how it was going to work, and what he needed from her. Li was more than willing to do her part, she even enlightened him to another way they could steal from the unsuspecting victims, right out of their bank accounts via wire transfer. The fraud was simple they needed to establish dummy accounts in either the names of a bogus businesses or individuals. All which were fairly elementary tasks for Li. When she joined the FBI, a part of her training was in fraud detection. Credit cards, personal and business accounts, check fraud, identity theft, domestic and international wire fraud, were all areas that she'd worked in her first year at the bureau.

"If you want my opinion baby I think the wire transfer will pan out to be much more profitable. Depending on the size of the account, there's literally no limit to how much could be transferred. I've seen cases where people have stolen millions from one account."

"How did they get caught?" he said intrigued.

"They got caught the same way most of them do baby, leaving trails. With that, much money involved, they get excited way too fast. Which usually leads to stupid mistakes that they wouldn't normally have made. You have to realize, a person who's capable of executing a crime of this magnitude has to be a professional, so they don't make that many mistakes. And when they usually do it's always towards the end when they've almost completed the job and can taste the money. So what the FBI does is they track those sorts of crimes backwards. Ninety percent of the time these cases are solved before they can even get to the beginning." Key was absorbing every word; he couldn't help but to respect her mind knowing that the best leaders were the ones who understood the concept of surrounding themselves with individuals who were actually 'smarter than they were,' thus keeping them informed as well as elevating their game. She was definitely bottom chick material, the kind of bitch that complemented real pimping and assisted it in its quest at looking first-rate. Many men would have been intimidated by the idea of having action at such a woman, but not Key he was reared and laced by some of the best pimps and players the game he had known. So he not only understood what he had, but was also able to grasp the bigger picture of what had been presented to him today – "why settle for crystals when you can have diamonds."

Chapter Four

For a whore operating without an established clientele, no stable place to lay her head, and the inability to retain and execute game on her own, life on the streets could be brutal. If good fortune didn't meet her half-way she'd starve and ultimately be swallowed up by the game like a wounded animal in the Safari Dessert. Since being fired by Key; her existence and whoring was worth no more than a couple hundred dollars a day at best. Paris had grown accustom to the best of the best; five-star meals whenever she caught the taste and shopping was only a matter of naming the place, king sized beds to lay in, and luxury vehicles to play in had become a way of life. Now here she was not even a week later eating low level dinning and sleeping in base model hotel rooms. After cursing herself for the self-inflicted wound, she retrieved the hotel room phone from the nightstand to call Key.

"I need to talk to him again, hope he answers," she said speaking to aloud. After a few rings, he picked up.

"Hello." Hearing his voice brought a sense of security and comfort to Paris, there was a lingering hesitation before she spoke.

"Hello," he repeated in an impatient tone.

"Hey," she finally said, unsure of how he would respond after discovering who was on the other end.

"Say punk hoe I thought I told you to lose my number. What the fuck you calling me for bitch?" Key said in a piercing voice after immediately recognizing who she was.

"Baby don't hang up on me please. I'm sorry I swear I had nothing to do with Red getting killed; I would never...." Bombarded with images of his friend laying stiff with his brains splashed all over the front seat of the Benz drove him from irritation to complete rage.

"I don't wanna hear that sorry shit buzzard! Do you realize what the fuck has happened on account of yo' game playing bitch?" He paused for a brief second as if he was waiting for a reply. "Yea I didn't think so. Aye, check this out fag you call this phone again and I'm gonna make you wish you died as easy as my homie did," he said tapping the end button on the cell phone.

"But Key I....." Her pleading was in vain, he was gone.

After hanging up Paris received a call on her cell phone from a potential client looking to set up a date. She quoted him a price tag of five hundred dollars for a full-service session, which entailed whatever he desired, and he agreed to meet her at the hotel in an hour. Normally she would have never agreed to such terms, but desperate times called for desperate measures and she hadn't touched that kind of money at one time since she'd been exiled from Key's stable. The clientele that Venus, Key's bottom hoe had set up for her would've been happy to have gotten a decent blow job for three-fifty and if they wanted pussy with it the bill could easily have ran into the thousands, depending on the patrons' finances. But her access to them had been extinguished and right now five hundred was enough to pay up her room for the week as well as provide her with a little extra pocket change. It was called survival, a downgrade that every whore would at some point experience in her career if she stuck around the game long enough.

Early morning hours at the LaQuinta Inn were usually quiet on week nights; with an occasional patron moving about through the hotels' lobby; anyone who walked by could hear the small radio that the clerk had playing on the lower shelf of the main desk. He was a jazz man, but preferred rock at work simply because it helped him at staying awake during the graveyard shift. Glancing at the clock, he became disappointed after realizing that there was still three hours left on his shift. "Six o'clock isn't coming fast enough," he thought to himself before focusing back on the funny section of the newspaper in front of him. Reading an episode of The Boondocks, he barely noticed when the short Mexican man came through the entrance sliding doors. It was only as they were just about to close did he look up to see who'd come in, and by this time it was too late he'd already turned down the hallway leading to the elevators.

The ride up was exhilarating, with thoughts of how he enjoyed the last little petite blonde-haired woman from the Airport Lounge Gentleman's Club. Oh, how he hoped this one was just as good, Hector had a fetish for the small figured white All-American types. For him, procuring these prostitutes seemed to be the only recourse left in sustaining what slight hint of man-hood he possessed. After being beaten and raped in a federal prison near Louisville, KY by a vicious group of Neo-Nazi affiliates, the lens that he viewed himself through would be forever altered. But visits with slutty white whores served as his therapy and it also gave him an outlet at sweet silent retribution. His mind transmitted back and forth from past to present; he could still smell the rapists sweaty cocks and balls against his nose, something that enraged him yet aroused his sexual lust as well. Just as his brain turned to the current channel and a pictured of Paris soothed his inner fury the elevator bell rang breaking him from the trance. When the doors open, he preceded left in search of room 301 while wiping away small beads of sweat that had formed on his forehead from the daydream/nightmare on the way up. As he came closer to the destination his mood intensified, a regular occurrence through repetition that had now seemed as normal as brushing ones teeth in the morning.

Paris was inside taking a swift hoe bath when she heard tapping at the room door. Elation was an understatement, she wasn't sure he'd show, but at five hundred an hour she was more than eager to give him his full money's worth. Before answering, she stopped near the bed to check on the straight razor she'd tucked under the pillow. Security was imbedded in her from the beginning by Venus and it was one thing she vowed not to stray away from after her and Chrissy faced an encounter in Chicago with a sadistic trick that got off on beating and strangling prostitutes with leather whips. After the inspection, with one last look in the mirror and satisfied by what she saw the young harlot gave herself a few inner words of encouragement. "I don't need no nigga, I can do this by my muthafuckin' self, let's get this money" she said, placing a plastic smile on her face on the way to the door.

Looking through the peephole she answered, "Who is it?" Before he could utter words, she unlatched the safety lock and opened the entrance wearing nothing but a lace red top and thong under a transparent knee-high robe. Placing her arm across the doorway she said, "Hello sweetie I guess you wanna come in?"

Hector stood bright eyed and silent, scanning her slender frame he simply nodded his head. She laughed and stepped aside permitting entry.

Inside she wasted no time, after a brief assessment of the client, she presumed him to be legit. Usually she'd conduct a brief session of dialogue to sniff out any police stings, but this guy's lust level was written all over his face. In no way could Hector conceal his perverse excitement. "Money, want money" he said in broken English form as he motioned the five crispy bills towards Paris.

This brought about the pleasure and delight she had been seeking, grasping for her earnings she said, "Thank you papi, I hope you came ready to enjoy your night in Paris?" while stroking his hand and leading him to the bed. When he sat down, she instructed him to lie back on the bed. "Mama knows what you like daddy," she said extracting his erect penis. For a moment, laughter nearly seized her after examining its full size. But that was irrelevant, in fact it made for an easier job; in the past she'd ran into some joints the size of miniature table legs and didn't too much care for the agony of wrestling with one of those that early in the morning. After slapping the small Lifestyle condom on, she was able to devour the entire stem down her esophagus all in one short stroke. And as she tickled the top of his nuts with her tongue, she hummed in unison with each blow of the humorous piece. Once certain that he'd been fully entertained by her concert; with a doctors touch; she lightly made her way through his pants pockets which were now pulled completely to his ankles touching the floor. Subsequent to the finding of more cash, she performed a quick set of movements, all in one motion, which entailed her rising up, bumping and slightly lifting the mattress to slip the cash inside, while she mounted herself to ride him. A routine that had took months to master, another piece of game that she discovered in the mist of Key's stable.

A few minutes into the act, she paused briefly to inspect the condom for damages, on her way, back up he requested the doggy style position. An idea that any seasoned hoe would immediately reject, the price for such a mistake could be fatal depending on the true intentions of the trick. The number two rule in the "Whores Manuel" was "to never willingly put yourself at a disadvantage," and to have ones back turned to a date was equivalent to telling a burglar when you'd be going on vacation. But against her better judgment and she propped down on all fours figuring it'd assist him in cumming sooner.

His self-containment went out the window as he pushed up against her rear; she talked nastier than any whore he had been with, *a real slut this bitch is*, he thought, while increasing the impact of each thrust. The harder he pounded the louder she became, with movements and words devised in such a shrewd manner that made it impossible for a sucka' to detect the theater. Nonetheless, it played heavy on his ego, so strong to the point where she could actually see him smiling from the mirror in front of her on the wall.

He savored every moment, while caressing her pale waist he closed his dark eyes as the sweet scent of sex and DKNY perfume filled his nostrils, reminiscing on his first experience with a young harlot he attempted to revisit that night each time he found himself with another one. But no amount of sex could ever erase the horror of his manhood being stripped away from 'those men,' as he would say. At that very moment that embarrassment and vengeance snatched away his fulfillment. His light grip around her waist turned into an inescapable clutch and the thrust of passion now mimicked that of a violent serial rapist.

"Whoa daddy, I love a man with a strong grip but that's a little too tight, can you loosen 'em up for mama please baby?" Paris said in the most provocative voice. But he continued on ramming, by now he removed himself from the room with images of her body being his and him portraying "Big Dino," one of the men who left him scared that fateful night.

Recognizing his abnormally intense breathing, she glanced back up towards the mirror to assess his sudden change in behavior. With a demonist, look and blood shot eyes he spoke sadistically to her in his native tongue. "Dame esta perra cono, dame esta perra cono!!" repeatedly, which meant, "give me this pussy bitch." She was uncertain as to what he was saying, but the demeanor gave off an alert of danger to her instincts that said, "Get the hell out of here." When she attempted to raise her hips to break, free of his grip he became even more violent, destabilizing her with a huge left hook to the ribs.

"Aww ohh, let me up you motherfucker, let me up!" she groaned at a near windless whisper.

"Callate puta, esto es lo que quiere!" he screamed as he delivered a series of brutal blows to both her sides before spreading her ass cheeks open as far as they would go.

"NO, PLEASE NO, pleaseeee... Why are you doing this to me?" she cried out as loud as she could. But it was to no avail he had taken a pillow and pressed it up against the back of her head muzzling any outbursts that could possibly be heard by would-be rescuers. He forcefully laid one arm across the pillow before inserting his penis into her anus. She fought with every inch of her being to break free, but was no match for the stout twenty-seven year old. Once fully inside he proceeded to pound with such might that she nearly fainted from the pain. Releasing tears and sounds of anguish she drifted into a sadden state and became somewhat numb to her attacker. From the beginning, she'd known full well that eluding this part of the game was a slim to none chance. But the quest of financial accomplishment and greed wouldn't allow her to heed to the degree of danger in which she was exposing herself. Now her greatest fear had come to reality and instead of money, it was "life" that had taken priority over all else. So with that she did her best to calm her fear and emotions in hopes that it would all soon end.

~ ❖ ~

The night was still and any movement present was invisible to human eyesight or senses. He moved about through the quiet suburban street in Oak Creek Village dressed in a black jumpsuit and tennis shoes. The agent had driven through the entire area near his target a few times before finally parking two blocks north and heading on foot. This operation was known only to him and if discovered he'd have some major explaining to do to his superiors. Prior to reaching his destination, he stopped briefly for a moment to make sure he was up for the mission.

"What am I going to say if someone sees me? What if there's some extra security that I'm not aware of?" were both questions that he'd contemplated. Nonetheless, he would stay the course, after all, he was certain that his partner was up to some sort of unethical business with Keyshawn and he owed it to himself and the agency to find out. At first thought, he had a mind to bring up his suspicions with Bender but opted not to until he had attained something more concrete.

Upon reaching the apartment complex, he removed the tiny tracking device and magnet from his sweatpants pocket and activated all its features. Making his way around the front of the building to the rear he looked up towards her windows to see if any lights had been turned on in the last five minutes. Before approaching the parking lot, the agent flipped up his hood and conducted a quick scan of vehicles nearest to him in proximity. After determining that he was, in fact alone he quietly made his way around the lot towards Chan's car in stealth like form. The black Honda Accord sat low to the ground, making its upper wheel-wells easily accessible once one was in arms reach. Lying on his back with only half the upper body under the car, he placed the gadget onto the frame in an undetectable position and vanished as quickly as he had appeared.

Chapter Five

After her 6a.m. walk, Chan headed to the office to begin her day. There was much to be done in such a small amount of time; with top priority being the wire conversations - which Bender would surely be ordering from the district office in Madison soon. The conversations were the most damaging evidence in Key's case, and they were relaying on her eyewitness accounts of what she, as an agent would provide. Chan was convinced that everything went as planned their entire case would be in complete shambles. She still had some time to address the matter with Paris's whereabouts; Chan knew they would need her testimony for the grand jury in any proceedings before and after an indictment was issued. She had no concerns with the other girls in the camp they'd be coached through the entire process, but they had no way of controlling what Paris would do. A scornful woman could undoubtedly be a disastrous ingredient in this sort of situation; she had witnessed firsthand how advantageous it could be for a U.S. Attorney looking to score an easy conviction. The key was to locate her before the bureau did.

There was little she could actually do from headquarters; the system set-up to trace an employee's every move in and out of the office. So after tying a few loose ends she stopped to speak with Agent Daley briefly before leaving the office.

"Hey buddy, what's up?" she said.

"Oh, same ole' partner, putting together some paperwork that should have been done, I'm a little behind" he said, trying to sound normal as possible; still in disbelief over the discoveries he'd made of Chan's actual dealings with Keyshawn.

"Great, I've got a ton of it myself but before I get to it today I have a few out-of-office runs I need to make first. See ya' soon" she said waving on her way down the hall.

"A few runs huh, oh I just bet you do," Daley said to himself turning to his desktop.

~ ~

On her way down the elevator Chan bumped into her boss S.A.I.C Sidney Bender, they discussed the case briefly before he reminded her again that details needed to be wrapped up soon, as the matter would be turned over to the U.S. Attorney's office. Knowing she needed to get going and didn't have much time brought about an extra sense of urgency and uneasiness in her all at once.

In fear of being tracked, she elected to drive her personal vehicle, figuring it would also assist her in flying low-key during this risky journey. A couple blocks away from the parking structure, she began checking her rearview mirror then made a few quick twists turns before heading towards a one-way street leading to the freeway. Her ride was short and ended ten minutes north in the township of Whitefish Bay. Exiting the expressway Chan began scanning the area around her destination, which was a medium size coffeehouse that offered Wi-Fi connection. Prior to going in Chan slipped on a long brunette wig and sunglasses. At 10am, the place was thick with caffeine addicts chasing their morning down with the latest concoction the coffee giants had introduced to the market. "Nice and full in here hopefully enough for me to go unnoticed," she spoke softly to herself while navigating her way to a corner near the back of the establishment. Once settled in she opened the laptop and logged onto the bureau's network with Seth Bennis's username and password. Inside she discovered that erasing the wiretaps permanently was a fairly simple task, in fact all that was required were the badge numbers of the agents working that particular investigation. All agents ID numbers were public information, and were accessible to anyone within the bureau through legitimately by referencing the agents' name and profile sheet, thus making the job more tedious than complex. She went to the counter to order a large ice water before continuing.

T.A. was busy enjoying breakfast prepared by Angelic, his top breadwinner of the month. She had managed to take down fifty bands in under thirty days, with the bulk of it coming from a wealthy client she had on the East Coast. So he gave her the entire week off for two reasons, the first being her work ethic and secondly he had a new prospect on the hook that was looking pretty promising. He wanted Angelic around for a few days to demonstrate to the newbie the proper manner in which a hoe was to cater to a pimp. Angelic took great pride in her role and was honored to be the chosen one to carry out this task. She knew her actions and overall performance would be a major factor in the young squares' decision to either link-up with their family or shy away altogether. Her reception of the newcomer was warm and welcoming; some of the most seasoned hoes in the game lacked this ability. To separate her emotions and contain jealousy meant that she possessed a stomach that the average bitches only wished she was blessed with. Another reason why T.A. selected her to execute the job over the others.

"Baby, I wanna go to Jazz In the Park later on today, its suppose to get up to 90 degrees and this will be one of the last nice days of summer," Angelic said looking at him.

"Cool, I told you this is your week and you can do whatever you want baby, so y'all go ahead and enjoy yourselves," T.A. said munching on a piece of bacon.

"You're not gonna go with us? I wanted to spend some time with you today," she said.

"Naw, we'll do something after you come back, besides don't you wanna get better acquainted with your new wife-in-law?" he said with a half of a grin.

"I guess," she said playfully looking at Autumn.

"Aw girl you don't wanna hangout with me? Forget you then," Autumn said laughing.

"I'm just messing with you boo," she said laughing. "We'll have a good time, plus we may catch some action shit. Which reminds me, baby we need to go shopping cause you know we gotta be looking the part" she was smiling now.

"You know where that money is and don't go crazy like y'all did last time." T.A. was referring to a seven thousand dollar shopping spree that three of his hoes went on in Chicago after he had given them the ok one morning in his sleep. But the truth of the matter was he didn't give a fuck and they knew it, his firm commanded sixty thousand a month at a minimum and he prided himself on the entire family looking as such.

"Come on bitch, let's get dressed so we can go do what stomp-down hoes do best! Make money and look good while we spending some, ya' feel me!" Angelic said laughing on their way to her bedroom.

T.A. glanced around the condo and pondered the motivation and level of commitment Angelic had shown since he'd knocked her a year earlier. She hadn't missed a beat from day one she'd given the family her all. "Here it is I give the bitch the week off and she still on automatic! That's a real live-wire hoe fo' ya' mane! What better life can a man live than the one I wake-up to everyday, only if these lames knew – they'd kill to be me." Just then, the ringing of his cell phone interrupted T.A.'s thoughts. After a few rings, he answered.

"Yeah?" he said

"I'm in the lobby homie, buzz me up," a voice said on the other end.

"Okay"

T.A. had been expecting his arrival all morning. They had some very important issues to discuss that couldn't wait. So when he knocked on the door he instructed the girls to remain on the upper level until the guest left the residence. He opened the door.

"Tiahmo what it is baby?" he said with a firm shake of the hand and a brief shoulder embrace.

"Same shit different day playboy," he said entering the threshold, "You got something to drink in the fridge? I'm thirsty as hell."

"Yea, it's orange and apple juice in there, go grab you something man."

Tiahmo was a long time comrade of T.A. and the Smith family; tall in stature with an almost harmless boyish presence, you would never suspect him for whom he really was in a million years. But make no mistake about it, the soft-spoken kid was extremely dangerous and he possessed the heart of a fearless lion. Bred on Atkinson since birth, the 19 year old had been an affiliate of the younger Smith's, Jaleal, and Marquis since grammar school at Green Bay Elementary. In essence, he was family/blood to them, thus making him ready and willing to do whatever necessary to protect his lifelong kinfolks. He was one of those young nigga's that you didn't want to fool around with unless you were willing to spend days on end laying in bushes until you tracked down and eliminated him. If you had not he surely didn't have a problem transforming you or your family into a horror story on the local news. This low-tolerance/no-nonsense type of attitude earned him undisputable respect amongst not only his peers, but also anyone who knew how he got down when it came to drama in the streets. Those closest to them knew that T.A. had played a huge part in molding Tiahmo into the young assassin that he would ultimately became today. In fact there were very few people whom TA actually trusted to bring on-board in matters of this capacity, and young

Tiahmo was number one on his list of go to guys, hands down.

When Tiahmo returned to the living room, T.A. didn't waste any time going right into details.

"So give it to me mane, what more do we know about these cats?" T.A. said referring to the White brothers.

"Well for starters, locating them wasn't easy bro. But we made it happen I got addresses on all three of 'em. Vance even found out where their mom's at." (Vance was another one of TA's young soldiers who meant business when it came to the murder game.) "These punks answering for Red homie," Tiahmo said shaking his head, he looked up to Red just as much as he did T.A.; they all had a hand in rearing him in his street sense.

"You know that's not even a question baby boy, it's just a matter of working out the details and a plan that will remove them all in one sweep." From there they began reviewing strategy.

Daley positioned himself three blocks down on the opposite side of the street facing the coffee house entrance in one of the bureaus low-key vehicles. The car was heavily tented, making a great shield for the hi-tech digital HD binoculars he utilized during the stakeout. They were equipped with 3D video recording capabilities, which the agent took full advantage of. The picture range and clarity were so superb that he could view the cheese and sesame seeds on a sandwich one of the patrons devoured over what appeared to be a business meeting of some sort. In nearly an hour of observation Daley hadn't seen Chan once, however he knew she was inside. Her vehicle was on the scene and the tracking device was in real-time. So he'd just have to remain patient.

The door slung open with an older late fifties or early sixties gentleman holding it for his wife. Seconds later Chan emerged moving hastily toward her car. He trailed her at a safe distance for the remainder of the morning. Following some pits stops at her bank, a post office, and a pharmacy; she led him on a short ride back on the expressway heading north again. When they exited, Chan drove one block before pulling up to strip mall and entering a local eatery for lunch.

Daley observed with great diligence as the customers came and went. He found it quite odd that she would choose to go this far just to have lunch alone, and figured she had to be meeting someone. After all, it was the perfect location for a person seeking a discreet gathering, of what was sure to be an illicit act of some sort.

It didn't take long before Keyshawn arrived driving a white Chevrolet Tahoe, Daley spotted him turning into the lot as he himself sat across the street in a credit union parking lot snapping photos with the binoculars. After he found a spot and parked, Keyshawn put on a pair of sunglasses before leaving the vehicle and casually strolling toward the restaurant door with the agent taking several more shots of him until he made his way out of view.

Inside Chan sat off to the side in the back as usual. When he arrived, she had already ordered their lunch, two lean corn beef sandwiches with sodas and chips. She looked up from the magazine briefly, as he was approaching and took his seat.

"What's the matter baby you look worried?" she said glancing through its classified contents.

"I'm good, so anything new?"

"Yes, I was able to get into the system and do what I spoke with you about."

Relief exposed itself upon his face when she told him the great news. "Is that so? Well good job baby girl!" he said with a pleased smile and a slight stroke of her hand, "So now what?"

"Well, now they have no audio and I'm the governments greatest asset, along with the other agents who are working the case of course," she said just as the waiter had arrived with their food.

When he left Keyshawn began, "What kind of information do you think you can get me on the White brothers' whereabouts?" he said paying special attention to her outer reaction to his request. Although she had now joined the dark side; as they said in Star Wars, there was still that part of him that was reluctant on asking her to do certain things. Especially something of this magnitude, he understood that Chan knew full well what he'd intended on doing with the information that she would provide to him in regards to the Whites. Murder had no reset buttons and witnesses were for life. However, her response came as quick as he asked.

"Yes, I can get you whatever you need baby that's not a problem, in fact I'll have something together for you by this evening," she said without a stall of a word, nor a blink of an eye providing him with total assurance that the plot was safe with her. Prior to today he'd never reveal anything that serious to a female he was dealing with, for fear that she eventually one day turn him in out of vengeance and scorn. But in this case that was a different; she actually had more on the line than he did not to mention the fact that she'd be directly involved herself.

"What about that bitch Paris? I think her bum ass might try to stick it to me if she had the chance. And that can't happen, you feel me?" he said looking her directly in the eye.

"Yeah, baby I understand."

"I just need to figure out exactly how precise the method in which to execute an approach that will look clean, can't afford to give them any lead way" he said glancing around as if he was pondering in difficulty.

"Baby don't worry about that, I promise you she won't be able to hurt you in any way. I'll take care of it," she said with a look of declaration.

The idea of him not having a plan of action in place to deal with a slow bitch of Paris's caliber was so far from the truth it wasn't even funny. But he threw the idea at Kimmie strictly because he knew she'd volunteer her services, and more importantly it would permanently attach her into his web had she decided to all of a sudden get a change of heart one day.

Key's intellect operated with alacrity, an attribute that he'd been blessed to have from a tender age in childhood, and over the years he was learning more and more just how to utilize this powerful trait in its entirety. He knew when to press someone and when to pause, and he toyed with his subjects from time to time in an effort to see how skilled he really was. It was one of the young pimp's youthful pleasures.

~ ❖ ~

The meeting/luncheon went rather quickly when they surfaced again Daley was still in the same spot eating a Big Mac value meal from McDonalds while reading the sports section of the newspaper. When she pulled out of the lot, he proceeded to trail all the way back to the bureau building.

Chapter Six

After the meeting, Keyshawn stopped by his mother's place to see her before she flew out of town for the weekend to visit his grandma. As he was coming through the front hallway, he could hear Keysha whispering something to Brandon in the living room. When he approached them his twin attempted to suppress the smirk she had on her face, but he knew her all too well.

"Y'all ain't fooling nobody and girl you know yo' ass can't hold water you just gave it away smiley," he said jokingly.

"What you talking about dude? Wasn't nobody doing nothing, we just chilling," she said blushing. Brandon had his faced glued to the TV as if he wasn't paying attention.

"And look at him, haha, that's terrible acting bruh."

"Huh," he said trying to appear dumbfounded

"Mannn both of y'all get the heck outta here," Keyshawn said, and instantly they all busted out in laughter.

"Yea, you gone have to do better than that B, I'm too savvy for that homie."

"Boy, whatever mind ya' business, mind ya' business," Keysha said laughing again.

"Haha, yea I just know you better not end up in front of no real detectives with that weak act speaking of which, what's up with your case B?" he said sitting on the leather recliner next to them.

"Well they want me to cop a deal for the two years still, I think I'm gonna do it, I can't beat the case Key. After we lost the "Search and Seizure" motion it was pretty much a wrap bro."

Keyshawn knew that Brandon had gained some education of the law since the case, because when he was first charged he didn't know anything about what was going on and thought they were about to give him a hundred years for the few pounds of weed he was pinched with.

"Yeah well that two aint bad, you'll be out in a year or less mane don't even trip."

"Oh, I'm not worried I really just want to get it over with now Key."

"I feel you, aye how long y'all been here? Is mama in her room?" he said switching the subject to the real reason he would come there.

"Yea, she just went in the basement before you came in," Brandon said focusing his attention back on Keysha. Her head laid in his chest, thinking about how life would be without him around was saddening to her. This was the first real relationship she had experienced and it killed her that he would soon have to leave. Brandon stroked her hair and she wrapped her arms around him tightly as they continued watching TV. Neither said a word, but through affection, they both knew exactly what the other was thinking.

~ ❖ ~

Michelle was in the laundry room putting clothes in a basket when he stepped off the staircase. She thought he was Keysha when he walked in.

"Girl... Oh hey baby I thought you were your sister, you know both of y'all walk as light as your grandmother. Where you coming from, you hardly ever come over this early in the day?" she said turning around with the clothes in her hand.

"I had to meet somebody for lunch ma' and I figured I'd stop by and see you before you left today," he said leaning in to kiss her on the cheek.

"Awww that's so sweet of you son, now would you grab this for me, your mama's getting old," she said smiling.

"Stop it ma' you ain't getting old, well at least not yet anyway haha." He took a hold of the bin and they headed into a sitting area that Keyshawn had remodeled for her when they bought the place. It was fully furnished with imported fittings from Italy. The entire basement was gutted wall to wall and equipped with the finest of everything down to the light fixtures and carpeting.

"I see Keysha has practically moved in huh?"

"Not really, you know her and that boy comes by every day. She ain't gone know what to do with herself when they send him away," she said shaking her head as she began folding the garments.

"Yeah, I know, but he'll be alright"

"And it doesn't help with what she's going through thinking about your father."

Keyshawn cringed every time the mention of "Tim" or "Dude" as he called him was brought up. They had yet to tell him about Tim's current battle with cancer, so he simply figured Michelle was referring to their dad doing another one of his pop-up visits and disappearing again.

"Well she'll get over it ma', that's why I always tell her to stop putting so much faith in dude when he comes around, and maybe she won't be torn so much when he leaves you know."

Michelle started to respond to his comment but elected not to only because she didn't care to debate the matter before she left town.

"You know how she feels about that man, nothing will change that Keyshawn. I just wish he hadn't told her about the cancer though, it's torturing that girl on the inside," Michelle paused for a moment to gather her thoughts.

"Cancer?" he said puzzled. Arriving back in the moment, she realized that they hadn't told him yet.

"Yes baby, Tim has cancer. He came here to tell you and your sister before he passes away; they've given him a few months to live."

A part of him was screaming, "Who cares? Fuck that chump! Now he wants to come around crying like a bitch because he got cancer. Fuck 'em let him die!" All those thoughts came in an instant, but he was raised to have empathy and compassion even for his enemies. So that led him to find a warm spot of some sort for the poor guy.

"Wow, that's messed up ma', I actually feel bad for the dude. Did they say exactly how long?"

"Not long, he's just now saying something but it's possible he's known this for a while knowing him," she said with a look of shame mixed with pity.

Not saying a word, he stared at her blankly. Even though he felt sorry for Tim, concern wasn't something that he really felt for him at the moment and he wasn't about to act like he had any either. Michelle knew her son and his thoughts better than he knew himself; therefore, she could only imagine what ran through his brain during those seconds of silence.

"Now baby, me and your aunt Hazel had a talk about all of this the day we had those words, and I understand that I can't make you feel anything. I'm sorry that he's not the person he should be"...

"Ma' what you apologizing for? You haven't done anything, you always...: He stopped himself before the conversation could get any worst, this isn't what he was here for and he wasn't about to let it spoil his mother's trip. "Look ma' I know, but you don't have to apologize ok," he said placing his hand onto hers. She looked at him.

"Baby just promise me that whatever your feelings are for him that you won't allow them to interfere with what your sister may be going through, ok? That's all I ask."

"No problem ma', I won't," he said with his signature smile.

"Okay, thank you baby."

"Alright, come on ma lets go get you ready for your flight. Who is taking you to the airport?"

"You are," she said laughing as they advanced towards the stairway.

~ ❖ ~

Reaching the cross section Keyshawn noticed a lingering vehicle as it turned off his mother's block into oncoming traffic. With the current events, he was extra careful at observing his surroundings. Immediately as he exited the driveway he spotted the two occupants in the four door gray Oldsmobile Alero. Although neither looked familiar, he still looped the block once before setting off to drop Michelle to the airport. However, when they finally made it around the car was gone and the block was as quiet as Cathedral Square on a Sunday night.

Chapter Seven

Attendance had easily gone into the hundreds as farewell wishers gathered one last time to say their final good-byes to Devin (Red) Highshaw. The memorial service looked more like a high school homecoming with all the young people in the church. Inside the pastor held the entire room captive as he delivered a powerful sermon as Red's mom Joyce sat in the front row staring into what she wanted to be a dream. Here she was burying her son at the age of nineteen, the only thoughts that were clear to her was the idea of her and Devy as she called him; living well beyond the present and him providing her with grandchildren whom she could one day give all the things to that she wasn't able to provide for her son. Joyce had been in bed since the day she received the call about his murder, sleeping only a few hours out of each one. Her heart was crushed in a million fragments, and life would, as she knew it now meant less and less each moment that she continued to live it. In fact, prayer was her only recourse and even that didn't seem to work.

Pastor Yancy Clemons stared into the rear of the building scanning the youth. In retrospect, he related to them, as he himself had not been long since removed from the street life. It was only after the death of his own brother that he chose to redirect his life onto the Lord's path. And looking at young Red only re-confirmed and assured him that he'd in fact made the right decision. He wanted to talk to them for God while he had the chance.

"I know a lot of you may think that you have no other choice! You might think that the game is your only way out of the ghetto-to-ah! But I'm here to tell you, that's right you," he said pointing to a young man sitting near the podium. "I wanna tell you that God didn't intend for you to live this way, he didn't intend for brother, Devin to die before his own mother and grandmother," he said glancing at Joyce and her mother Maxine.

When he spoke to them Maxine reached for her daughter she didn't have to say a word, because the pastor's said all that she felt at the moment. She held onto her in silence as he continued on with his sermon. Maxine too hadn't yet completely wrapped her mind around the idea of her grandson being gone. It almost delivered her into a stroke-like state when she looked at him lying in the casket. All she could do was hope and pray that he was with the Lord, thinking that gave her a slight form of peace within.

A few rows behind them were, Keyshawn and his family along with T.A. and the Smith immediately behind them. There wasn't a dry eye in the section as they all listened to the pastor, who was now beginning to lead the choir in song.

Key's thoughts drifted back and forth between the past and present. Red was the first person in his life whom he had considered to be a friend. He cried heavily to himself, regretting the fact that they allowed themselves to slip so hard. "I shoulda' been on point for us man," he said blaming himself.

Keysha leaned in closer to him as she heard the whisper, "It's gone be ok bro," she cried rubbing the tears from her twins face.

T.A. sat back in deep thought the streets had never dealt them a blow that penetrated their immediate circle in such a manner. All he could envision was blood, bodies, and more blood. He rose-up to step away for a brief moment. "Excuse me," he said to one of his younger cousins who were sitting next to him at the end of the row.

When the phone rang, all was quiet and each ear was attentive to the signal. "Hello," casually said the receiver.

On the other end, he didn't utter a word before closing the flip phone and ending the call.

"Ok y'all know what's happenin', everybody knows their positions, now let's move," Tiahmo said directing the young troops. They were all strapped and dressed for the occasion, breaking off into three separate groups heading for specific targets.

After placing the order, he stood near the curb to breathe for a second before returning to the service. One couldn't know what losing someone that close could do to them until it actually happened, and he vowed to do all that he could to prevent it from re-occurring if at all possible.

On his way back in he spoke to Apple and Cinnamon; both of Red's front-runners they were embracing each other off to the side near the entrance consoling one another. Huddled up near-by was a small squad of local and international pimps who would come to the funeral strictly to shoot their shots at the fresh widow wife-in-laws. T.A. made a mental note of putting a thorough checking on each of them when the time was right. He didn't want to cause any confusion in front of Red's family.

Back at his seat, he tapped Key on the shoulder, "You good homie?"

"Yea, yea, I'm cool T.," he said mustering up every inch of strength that he had left to compose the obvious lie. But T.A. knew it was killing him.

"Don't trip, they won't get away with this one lil pimp," he said looking at Red in the casket.

On the other side of the isle the undercover agent held the black bible with its spine upright and facing towards their section in hopes of catching good enough footage where an analyst at the bureau could dissect some of the conversations through lip movement.

Chapter Eight

Throughout history the upper east side of Milwaukee was home to arguably the best hustlers, the city had to present. Its geographical location sits between the north side, which houses most of the Blacks and the lower east side, which is mixed with Latinos, Whites, and other nationalities. In turn, this made for an overall diverse community, which happened to be the essential component of success for most of its young up-and-coming. However, amongst players it is common knowledge that there's abundance of young boppers who frequent the area that are lost and in dire need of direction, making it a scouting ground for potential prostitutes.

Today had been absolutely gorgeous and Fox was out in pursuit exercising his game. He wasn't originally from the East but his mom lived near Holton and Center streets for the past decade and by visiting her he'd become somewhat attached to the neighborhood. After leaving her home, he stopped a few blocks away at Lil General a local convenience store to grab a pack of cigarettes. On the way out his antennas immediately went up after spotting a tall slim young hottie across the way near a check-cashing establishment. He quickly jumped in the black Mercedes; took his best cologne out the glove box for a shot then checked his diamond studded Chloe frames before pulling up and springing into action.

"What up wit' it shawty?" he said cruising slowing along busy MLK Dr. The girl looked at the whip an abruptly recognized Fox. In the game, a player's vessel was his signature and most often than not in the pimp lane, it meant all the difference, an understanding that Fox was able to grasp in his earlier stages of the streets well before he entered the services business. She turned away and sped-up. But the veteran wasn't gonna let her off the hook that easy.

"I know you know who I am, Fox the P.," he said with arrogance. "Let me help take you out that nightmare most muthafucka's call living baby." She glanced over her shoulder then hastily towards the rear of his vehicle.

"No thanks, I'm straight." Her body language caused him to check his rearview mirror, and to his displeasure, he saw what appeared to be a green unmarked patrol car with a black and a white cop inside tailing him.

"Fuck," he said reaching for the 40-caliber, glock he'd placed on the passenger seat. Then after slipping it in the armrest and composing himself, Fox proceeded to make a left turn onto a side street to see if they would follow. They did and the passenger activated the cherry on the roof and hit the sirens.

"These chumps on some bullshit," he said pulling over to the curb. Fox was more agitated than worried he wasn't a felon and even if he was it wouldn't stop him from toting a pistol. Not only was he a player, but pure gangster as well he lived by the same motto that most conscious street nigga's did - "I rather be caught with it than without it."

By now, the two officers had exited their vehicle and were approaching with hands on the weapons. The first one to speak was the white cop.

"Sir will you please unlock the door and get out of the car with your hands up?" Fox began to wonder why they were ordering him out of the car without just-cause however still did as he was told.

"Officer may I ask what did I do?" he said with a puzzled look.

"We'll tell you about it in a minute, put your hands behind your back," said the black cop who stepped in to cuff and lead him towards the squad car.

"Aye, man what kinda shit is this tell me something," he said while being put inside. Realizing that they were now getting ready to pull off he began to think that maybe he had done something that was now catching up to him.

"Alright what's the deal? Y'all got me, now what the fuck did I do?" he said out of frustration.

"A detective downtown wants to talk to you, just relax we'll be there shortly" the driver said looking at him through the mirror. Fox didn't respond, he'd done so much dirt he couldn't even begin to figure out what this may have been about. He laid his head back on the seat and rested his eyes as they were now entering the freeway heading towards the station.

On the south side of town at a property that his older sister owned, a thick dark skinned stallion by the name of Whitney was entertaining Profit. When he wasn't pimping part-time he liked to indulge in casual sex with females whom the game deemed as squares, and to pimps that was a complete no-no. It was actually a cardinal sin to freak with any woman who hadn't broke bread with pimpin' but more and more the game was seeing the rule being bent because there'd been a rush of pretenders toying around with the life. In a world with beautiful women everywhere, you turned one must have a special discipline about himself, an attribute that Profit lacked from the start.

As he lay back on the bed propped up on his elbows, his new friend Whitney slowly wiped her body all over in baby oil. He'd met her only a week prior at North Ridge mall in a store she cashiered at called Merry Go Round, and for the entire seven days he'd just been dying to see her gigantic ass in the flesh.

"Square bitches are the biggest sluts," he mumbled to himself while giggling all at once.

"You like that don't you?" she said bending over in his face touching her toes. Now preoccupied with looking up her skillfully trimmed camel toe, he had the slightest clue of what was going on behind him. When the cold tip of the silencer met the back of his skull, Profit knew what was next. He may not have been able to see his assassin but his entire life was right there in front of him, he began pleading.

"I don't know what this is about homie, I'm a pimp I don't fuck wit nobody" as he was finishing his sentence the play suddenly became clear to him. His friend Whitney so he thought was now standing in the corner looking at him seemingly without a care in the world. Oh how he now felt like the sucker he actually was. *"This punk bitch"* his mind flash a thought before getting back to the real matter at hand which was preserving his life.

"Whatever the beef is my people will pay to have it squashed, I swear on my life," he said trying to remain calm.

"Bill Gates can't pay yo' way outta' this one fag ass nigga, this for Red pussy" the man behind the voice was Tiahmo when Profit heard those word his eyes opened wide as Lake Michigan. He tried to say something but was muted at the first syllable by Tiahmo's right trigger finger. He pumped three bullets through his head in an instant. When he finished Tiahmo walked around to look at Profits face. Blood quickly began flowing all over the bed.

"I should decapitate this mog and mail his fucked up face to his mama," he said to a crony. No one replied the other two were ready to complete their mission and leave. Whitney was in the corner nearly in tears now shaken from the coldness of the murder and the fact that it didn't affect the killer one bit.

"What you over there shaking for bitch?" he said clutching the handle tighter.

"Tiahmo I'm scared, I did what you asked can I please go now?" she said heading closer to panic.

"Sorry baby, no witnesses," he said pulling the trigger twice and hitting her in the chest. As her body hit the floor, he walked over and hit her in the center of the chest once more. When he looked up they were both staring at him.

"What? I didn't wanna hit her in the face. Come on let's get outta here," he said as they all filed towards the door.

As the cars speed decreased Fox opened his eyes instinctively. He scanned the area wondering why they had passed up the exit leading to first district.

"I thought you said I was going downtown," he said looking back and forth at the two would-be officers.

"No, the detective want to see you at another location just be cool buddy were almost there okay," said the white gentleman.

They had gotten off in an area near Menominee Valley a few blocks north of the casino. All its landscape consisted of warehouses, factories, and industrial companies. The drive to the destination from the freeway exit was brief, and when the vehicle arrived to what appeared to be an abandon building the driver stopped at a huge garage entrance before they were able to gain entry.

In the back seat, Fox was beginning to question these guys' true identities, for a second he thought they may have been Feds especially when they pulled into the building and closed the steel door behind them. He could see that there were people at the back of the place but couldn't make out the images. They drove a few more feet before finally stopping at which time his door was opened and he was taken out. A man in handcuffs was being escorted by someone walking toward them. As the figures came close enough to them Fox could now see that the one in cuffs was none other than his brother Blake. His mind was racing ninety-thoughts a second now.

"Well, I'm glad to see you officers made it here safely," Tiahmo, said standing face to face with them now.

"Haha, get the hell out of here. How did that other thing go? " said the black one who Fox was now certain wasn't a cop said laughing. Both brothers starred at one another not saying a word, Fox had been around Blake long enough to know exactly what he was thinking. It was written all over his face, they had got caught slipping heavy and were both about to pay the piper.

"Everything is copasetic - homie checked out," he said looking at Fox. "Oh yeah, in case you ain't know he's talking about your other brother, we clipped him tryna' get a piece of pussy," Tiahmo said laughing. "He went fairly easy, but sad to say for you two it's not gone be as smooth. In fact, it's gonna be quit mess, sucks to be the older ones huh. Get them ready," he said then walked off.

The order "get them ready" was the term for them to be stripped naked, gagged, and chained to two steel tables. As they were uncuffed and ordered to strip, Blake put up a small fight that was to no avail. They both squirmed a bit as they were being chained, Fox had a look so fearsome on his face that Blake badly wished that he could've taken whatever pain they were about to endure all on his own. Before they could mentally prepare themselves for the agonizing surprise one of the men pulled two three feet poles with professionally sharpened tips on each end out of the trunk of a car, followed by several bats and began handling them out to everyone. Observing this Fox immediately went bananas he was trying to saying something all the while crying out to his soon-to-be attackers.

"What you say? I can't hear you," Tiahmo said before thrusting the long pipe up his anus. He screamed so deeply Blake began crying and they hadn't even touched him yet.

"Good thing we got a gag on him," Tiahmo said laughing again. "Well you should've thought about that before y'all order that hit on my homie," he said jamming the rod inside Fox again. This time the screams were much worst, he repeated the ritual a few more time before finally turning to Blake and administering identical treatment. Twenty minutes into it, the scene resembled that of a battle in the mist of the Civil War. They beat and sodomized the pair until both finally pasted out from shock and pain of the entire ordeal.

After leaving the bloody lifeless bodies on the slabs, General Tiahmo phoned T.A. with the same notification signal confirming that the assignment had been complete.

Chapter Nine

The following day Chan and Daley were summoned to an early meeting in regards to the White murders. A tipster phoned the MPD alerting them about the deaths T.A. wanted them found as soon as possible. In the streets, the only thing that demanded respect was "revenge" and he understood that there had to be a strong statement displayed for all in the game to see that his camp still meant business and were a dangerous forced to be fooled with. His assumptions were on point the manner in which the brothers were killed was so heinous that even some of the most ruthless gangsters questioned their method of violence. It was no secret who was behind the massacre, with Milwaukee being such a small city word spread fairly quickly when it came to things of that nature.

But whenever the streets spoke the words echoed beyond its element. There were thousands of informants and good Samaritans seeking to supply any form of information they could find that would possibly earn them a lighter sentence or a few extra dollars. By 7a.m every hotline and police phone in the city was jumping with hundreds of leads most of which were leading back to T.A. and Key. This infuriated Sydney Bender, who was now getting calls from the Mayor, Police Chief, as well as his superiors in Madison. The consensus was mutual; the investigations on Keyshawn Watson and T.A. Smith had to be closed immediately.

"We have no more time ladies and gentlemen, these people have gone completely mad, and it's starting to really make us look bad. Many think that the bureau is moving too slow on its investigation of these individuals, thus making for a relaxed environment that is enabling all of the violence that's surrounding our case," Bender said pacing the floor.

"Sir do you think we're ready?" Chan said appearing genuine.

"At this point agent we have no choice. We will go with what we have on these guys, all of which I believe is sufficient enough to put them away for a substantial amount of time. The grand jury is hearing the complaint this afternoon, and I'm sure we'll have indictments. Chan and Smith be sure to secure body attachments on these six, we'll need them this afternoon," he said pointing to pictures of Venus, Classy, Chrissy, Paris, Angelic, and Danielle. All were associates of T.A. and Key's stables.

Locating the girls wasn't a difficult task there'd been a standing order to trace all of their movements in and out of town for the past month now. Knowing they would need them for the grand jury, Bender took no chance at losing the girls agents throughout the country tracked them daily. Once warrants were I place they would simply have them picked up, hauled off to an airport, and flown back to Milwaukee within a couple hours.

"Okay, we don't have much time so let's get moving people. I want no excuses have them in this city no later than 1pm," he said putting his suit jacket on before heading to the door. Deadlines of this fashion were regular occurrences at the bureau, and he was sure things would be on schedule by noon. On the way out, he remembered one other thing.

"Oh yeah, Chan do we have any address or location on Ms. Tannery?" he said speaking of Paris.

"Yes sir, we have two possible addresses that I was able to find yesterday. One is what I believe to be her fathers' home. Neighbors have confirmed seeing her there several times last week," Chan said.

"Good I'd like you to be there when she's picked up; since you have a relationship with her I think we'll have a better chance of getting her to debrief right away. We'll resume here at noon folks, if anyone needs anything feel free to come to my office," he said rushing out the door leaving the agents hustling immediately behind him.

~ ❖ ~

Key had been up until four in the morning, they had thrown a party in Red's honor at the club following the repast, which had taken place at Red's grandmother's place. He was in a deep sleep when his cell phone began ringing at 7:32 am. He almost didn't answer until he rolled over and seen Keysha's throw away phone number on the caller ID.

"Yea, what's up sis?" he said in a groggy voice.

"Get up nigga don't nothing come to a sleeper but a dream!" aint that what you say, she laughed jokingly.

"I'm still tired girl, what yo' ass want this early?" he said stretching slightly.

"I talked to Patrice this morning and she wants to know if you will come see her with me and mom later?" Knowing what that signal meant he was fully awake almost instantly.

"Yea tell her I'll be there, what time y'all going?" he said getting out of the bed.

"We wanted to go now, because she's leaving tomorrow bro."

"Ok, let me get dressed quick and I'll be over there."

After hanging up the phone, Keyshawn gathered his thoughts for a brief moment. Him and Kimmie worked out various coded messages that were to be delivered through Keysha had anything gone wrong. The key phrase was "I talked with Patrice," which meant that Kimmie called and was warning him that things were closing in and Keysha's last sentence actually meant two things. One being that Kimmie wanted him to meet her at the secret place they had designated for this moment and the second part was notifying him that he needed to be extremely quick because there wasn't much time.

Within minutes, he was dressed and out the door in route to a low-key apartment, they shared not too far away. On the way over, he phoned T.A. to bring him up to speed, their conversation lasted all but thirty seconds and by the time he had hung up T.A. was also on the move to put his emergency plan in place.

By the time Keyshawn arrived, Kimmie was already there ready to give him the full spill. When he entered the dwelling, she was busy making several phone calls to various departments within the bureau. As he walked in she was standing in the living room discussing a time and place where she would be meeting U.S. Marshals to execute the search of a home in hopes of finding Paris. A search that would only lead them to a dead-end, because Chan knew that the intended target was in fact in Plymouth working in a cheap sleazy strip club at the moment. Before she hung up Key filled himself in by listening in on the conversations every word until she was finished.

"Baby I just left a meeting with my boss, they're seeking indictments today and they have agents going to grab the girls within the hour to bring them back here to testify in front of the grand jury," she said then paused for a moment.

"What the fuck! Already? I don't get it why so soon?" he said staring at the floor with his mind flipping through what seemed to be a hundred different scenarios.

"With those guys being found the way they were this morning we're getting pressure from all around us to wrap this up and bring everyone in baby," she said "But there's nothing to worry about as long as they refrain from saying that you acted as their pimp you'll be okay.

"Yeah I understand that, but what about that punk hoe Paris?" I'm sure they're looking for her as well," he said out of frustration.

"Don't worry about her; I supplied them with bogus addresses so they won't find her by today. If it goes to trial we'll have plenty of time to get to her," she said.

"Okay, cool," he said feeling a bit relieved.

"Well baby I can't stay any longer, I have a million things to do within the next few hours, and I'll be calling to keep you in tune with the status of everything. Just be sure to keep any and all illegal contraband far far away from you, they can pick you at any moment now and we don't wanna give them anything else."

"Right, right okay well I'll be waiting to hear from you," he said before walking over and kissing her on the forehead.

Chan left first and he was behind her five minutes later. As Keyshawn left the dwelling, Agent Daley was a block away rapidly snapping photos. He was now sure that what Chan had been doing behind his back and there wasn't a question that she'd just repeated what was told to her in the briefing that morning. Daley knew that something had to be done; her actions could put him or his colleagues in danger at this point. "She's left me no choice," he said before pulling out into traffic.

Chapter Ten

When Keyshawn drove up his twin was outside her apartment building awaiting his arrival. Before he called, her Keysha was preparing for a visit with Brandon at the House of Corrections. He took a deal for two years in state prison for the marijuana police found in his vehicle, but due to the pleas of countless staff and professors at University of Wisconsin Milwaukee the judge went below the district attorney's recommendation of prison and instead sentenced him to a year of county time followed by four years of probation. Everyone was relieved especially Keysha, she was madly in love with him and believed that he was an angel sent from heaven.

They spoke of Brandon briefly before reaching her unit. Once inside Keyshawn explained to her what she didn't know and made a request for her assistance in securing his most valuable possessions into safety before he was picked up by the government.

"Keysh' you cannot screw this up sis! I need you to take all this stuff to that safety deposit box that we set-up. These fags won't get all my shit, I'm keeping something if I go down" he said looking her square in the eyes.

"Damn bro., now you? They're about to take you away from me like they did Brandon," she said tearing up.

"Girl, ain't nobody taking me nowhere, I just need you to put those things up while I have the chance because if they find it I'm sure they won't let me keep the shit." He was right, Keyshawn had over a hundred and seventy thousand in cash stashed away at his condo, over a hundred thousand in jewels, and a sixty thousand dollar Mercedes not to mention a brand new Cadillac Escalade. The only thing he actually had a chance of maintaining was the money and jewels if he moved them quick enough. Everything else was already recorded and ordered to be seized upon arrest.

"Twin you just said, "If you go down," so you don't know what's going to happen. Why are they looking for you anyway, is it about those girls? If so they can't take a person to jail for that can they?" she was puzzled. Keysha was extremely book intelligent but when it came to knowing the law, she was clueless.

"That depends," he said before getting cut off.

"Depends on what bro?"

"Look sis, we don't have the time to discuss it right now, I'll explain it to you later. After you do take care of that we'll meet up and talk it over at lunch."

"Alright, we can go by mama's place."

"No, no, no we can't. Come on I need you to get moving, and don't forget to go see T.A.," he said before giving Keysha a hug to ease her mind. After she left Keyshawn relaxed on the couch to clear his thoughts and contemplate his next set of moves.

The time was 6:45am in Reno, Nevada most of the tourists were still up from the previous night running through casinos not concerned with time but how many black jacks or seven's they could score on the tables. As patrons strolled about in search of the latest thrill, Venus and Classy were on high alert hunting rich tricks with expensive jewels or long plastic. Their pursuit was quickly satisfied, as usual, after meeting two English businessmen from the U.K.

As they exited the Sands Regency, three black governments SUV's quickly swarmed the Lincoln Continental limousine before its driver was able to leave the parking spot. While putting the vehicle back in park four U.S. Marshals along with two FBI field agents approached securing all its doors.

"Sir, can you please turn off the engine, exit the vehicle, and sit over to the right here," said the tall slim agent.

The driver was bewildered his first thought was that he had done something wrong.

"Ah, is everything ok? What'd I do?" said the driver as he opened the door.

"Everything's fine sir won't take much of your time we'll be just a second here," said the agent again. Hearing those words of assurance, he was relieved and did as he was told.

By now everyone in the limo were near panic, except for Venus, she was sharp enough to know that this day would soon be coming. When the agents opened the door, one of the men immediately began singing.

"Officers we're so sorry, all we were trying to do was have a little of fun with these girls"

"Shut the hell up," the other man said with a look of disgust.

"First off sir I'm not an officer, I'm a federal agent with the United States FBI. I could bust you for that residue you have exposed on the console there but I'm here on a matter of greater importance," he said glancing at Venus then to Classy.

"Ms. Milton and Ms. Franklin would you both please exit the vehicle," he said moving out of the doorway.

Not fully awake to the situation Classy looked at Venus and was in the commission of saying something before she was stopped in mid-sentence.

"Ms. Milton, no talking just exit the car as instructed please," said the same agent.

Upon exit, both were separated and rushed away to a nearby airport where a federal jet was awaiting to fly them to Milwaukee.

Back in Wisconsin, agents seized Chrissy at the Holiday Inn hotel in the small township of Port Washington. She had been on an overnight call with one of her regulars from the wealthy River Hills community.

T.A.'s entire stable was nabbed along with two of his ex-hookers Agents' Smith and Daley detained Angelic at his east side condo on her way to the residents' exercise room. From his bedroom window, T.A. seen the heavily tinted black vehicles parked alongside the building seconds before they brought her out.

"Shit! Well here we go," he said before phoning Keyshawn to brief him on the latest developments.

Accompanied by Marshals along with two squads from the West Allis city police department, she stood at the door knocking for almost five minute before walking around to the rear of the house. As she was coming back around to the front, she noticed a short stubby elderly man who had been sitting across the street with a group of senior citizens approaching slowly. One of the officers was moving away from the house advancing toward the man but Chan cut him off before they connected.

"It's okay officer I'll handle it." The last thing she needed was for a nosy neighbor to come along and shed light on her staged operation.

"Hello sir, how are you?" she said with a doctored smile. The man acted as if he hadn't heard a thing she said as he went on to finish his mission of telling what he knew.

"I don't know who you people are looking for but that house has been empty for almost a year now," he said with a soft southern accent.

In efforts to conceal their conversation and to obscure his surveillance, she positioned herself directly between him and her associates before carrying on meaningless dialogue with him in regards to what he may have known. He told her that in fact the house had been occupied by a gentleman and his girlfriend for two years before they moved around ten months ago. He provided her with their descriptions, vehicle makes, etc. All of which were facts about Paris's dad that she had already known, thus the reason why she had chosen to go there. Had anyone investigated further they would have been able to confirm and it would have simply appeared as though she would had expired information. Once she'd lent him enough time to feel as though he'd contributed his part to society she brought the charade to an end.

"Okay sir, well I thank you kindly for your assistance, and if you hear or see anything else that you feel may help us here's my number for you to call okay?" she said smiling while handing him her card. The man responded with a nod before offering her his hand and walking away.

Chapter Eleven

Bender was on a call with the United Sates Attorney's office when Chan strolled in.

"One moment agent," he said holding up his left hands index finger. Chan walked over to a gang of plaques that he had been awarded for performing various services throughout his years at the bureau. Highly decorated, Sidney Bender was arguably the best choice for the S.A.I.C. position when it became available. He was thorough, diligent, honest, and fair among other things. Usually when there was a shift of power within an office of the agency there would be a host of agents and staff expressing the disapproval for the newly elected head. But not in the case of Agent Bender, he'd transitioned into the spot with ease.

When she could hear that he was about to end the call Chan turned toward the big oak desk and took a seat across her boss just as he was hanging up.

"I've gotten word that all subjects are in custody so we're ready to move forward. Now however, the U.S. Attorney has raised the issue of their detainments due to the manner in which it was all expedited. He's fucking calling me with this bullshit like I'm the guy who's putting the pressure on everyone here," he said throwing his hands in the air. "Excuse my language agent, sometimes I just can't stand the audacity of those assholes in Madison," he said taking a drink of water.

"No problem sir I totally understand, maybe you should consider seeking a position over there so you can change policy?" Chan said smiling.

"What are you trying to do humor me here? I'm comfortable where I am," he said with a light chuckle. It was the first time she had actually seen him this frustrated and using so much profanity and she had actually found it quit humorous.

"Anyway, how did everything go with the search for this other girl," he said leaning back in the huge leather recliner rubbing his temples.

''Not too good sir, the information I obtained was outdated, I spoke to a neighbor briefly and was told that the father had actually moved away from the house almost a year ago."

"Well I guess six out of seven isn't bad, but in the meantime see if you can get his any of his updated information."

"Yes sir, of course. What time will we be having the briefing?" Chan said. Bender glanced at the stainless steel Movado timepiece.

"We do it in the next half hour, so be sure to stay close by."

"Sure thing, before I go sir I have a question."

"What's that agent?" he said while tending to something on his computer.

"Do you think it would be necessary that I be the one to interrogate these girls?" he stopped what he was doing to consider her question.

"You know that actually might not be a bad idea, let's go with it. But of course you know the prosecutor may want to be present during your interrogation, keep in mind these people more valuable to us as witnesses than defendants."

"Yes they are, I'll see you at the meeting then," she said while getting up to leave the room. The idea of what he'd just said to her sent a chill through her body, she knew the bureau was about to do any and everything in its power to get the girls to flip it was they specialty thus being the central cause for their ninety-six percent conviction rate.

On the way out of Bender's office she was met by Agent Daley.

"Hey partner, I heard everything went as planned at Smith's place good job," she said with a head nod.

"Yeah I'm glad this is all coming to an end now, I'm ready to move on to something else ya' know."

"I know what you mean, well I guess the briefings going to be shortly I have a few things to finish before then, see you there buddy."

"Okay, and aye uh you think me and you can have a word when we're done there, I have some things I've discovered that I'd like to share with you," he said.

"Not a problem, see you then," She said as they both parted ways

Chan hadn't had any suspicions because she had no idea what Daley had been up to, she took his words for face value and continued on without a second guess.

By 10am, Keyshawn and T.A. had met up in the hood at Mr. Perkins Family Restaurant to discuss things further. The place was packed this time of day as usual, which was the reason they chosen to meet there. Being that it was such a small building the twenty or so patrons and staff seemed more like a hundred making for a noisy atmosphere loud enough for them to chat quietly over breakfast without being heard. T.A. was jittery, but Keyshawn had confidence in his Kimmie and believed that the worst wouldn't be as bad as T.A. thought it would.

"T I'm telling you homie you worrying too much," he said.

"Listen lil bro, I understand you got the bitch on lock and all, but to be quite honest pimp my concern is with them hoes they just grabbed mane. I'm not too sure all of them will hold up under that pressure. Key we talking 'bout the government here now, them people play dirty."

"I understand but you briefed them on everything thing didn't you?"

"Do a bear shit in the woods nigga? Of course I did, but that shit means nothing, none of them bitches have never been under that kind of microscope before blood. I don't trust that they care about a nigga that much too actually go to the can with a muthafucka' if need be my man."

"I feel you on that but all you can do at this point is look at it as a test, if the bitches stand up then that means all that allegiance they been pledging was the truth right."

"A test?! So you are looking at this as a chance for a hoe to prove herself right now?"

"Yeah, what better time than this T?"

"Say man, do you not understand how much time niggas facing right now dawg? I can dig where you coming from with the 'proving herself thing' but nigga we can't stand for them bitches to go left on us, the cost is too high playboy."

"True, but what can we do at this point but wait this shit out and let that bitch Kimmie work her magic. I think we good T., but if not then I hope you got one hell of a stash put up cause we might be there for a while." T.A. was listening but his better judgment had begun to kick in once his actually seen his women are snatched. He knew sometimes street women were built with firmer stomachs than a lot of the niggas who played the game. But still he disliked the idea of a hooker or anyone for that matter, being the deciding factor in whether he'd go to prison or not.

Chapter Twelve

The meeting lasted for a half an hour and was over by 11am. In addition to the bureau's agents and other staff was assistant U.S. Attorney Daniel O'Malley along with his junior associate Patrick Griffin. Areas covered were the key elements of the investigation that could be put together in two hours to be presented before the grand jury. Protocol requires that the Justice Department's prosecutor present witnesses (if any), evidence, and a simplified outline of the case to the grand jury when seeking an indictment.

On the way out Chan and Daley strolled to an empty conference room nearby. After they both were seated, he didn't waste any time getting straight to the point.

"So agent how long have you been straddling the fence?" he said looking her directly in the eyes.

Chan was caught completely off guard with his question, it showed all over her face when he asked her. But she did her best to remain calm.

"Straddling the fence? I don't understand what you mean partner," she said trying to appear confused.

"Oh, come on now you know exactly what I'm talking about Chan. I know you and that Watson guy have a thing going on and you're feeding him information from the bureau, I know you've been sneaking off having meetings with him even after your infatuation of his little string of whores was put to an end. Shall we start with your meeting at Froedtert hospital a few weeks ago? Real cute how you made sure no one seen you leave out together, so you thought that is. I was also there the other day when you two went on your outing at the corn beef place; you remember right after you left the coffeehouse. Do you need me to tell you what you had for lunch?" he paused.

Chan didn't say a word, the details he'd given her were overwhelming and there was no question that he knew exactly what he was talking about. As the silence grew, she began to feel sick.

"You don't look too well partner, oh tell me is it the baby?" he said with a smirk. That blow was worse than others were.

"Fuck he knows everything," she was thinking to herself. Then she began to look around at the people who were coming and going about through the hallway outside.

"You didn't think I knew that either huh? I actually can't believe you would stoop so low agent, I mean of all the people in the world to end your life and career over you picked this scum bag?" Daley felt a sense of betrayal, jealousy, and hurt all in one. He always had a thing for Li but never possessed the courage to tell her how he felt. To him Keyshawn was the lowest life form God had created, but to Li Chan he represented strength, manhood, and security. All of which were characteristics that any woman wanted in her man, sure he was a pimp and a drug dealer but her position in regards to that was that everyone had flaws and he was just a regular person striving to make a way out of the hand he was dealt. However, Daley on the other hand completely despised him, mainly for the same reason that most squares hated hustlers and players - they possessed certain gifts that they didn't and to an insecure man that could do some sever damage to his ego.

Daley continued with his ranting for about a minute until he realized what a fool he must have looked like by now. As he attempting to scold her Chan wasn't paying any attention to him, her next move was the only thought that played in her brain. For some reason as he was talking, she kept thinking that agents would be coming any minute now to cuff her and take her into custody. Daley could sense her paranoia.

"Just so you know I haven't told a soul, you see I'm not sure exactly what I want to do here. On one hand, I believe you should be put away with these animals. But on the other I feel a sense of shame and concern for you agent," he said all the while being conscious of his tone. That gave Chan a great relief, but could she trust it, could she trust what he was saying. For all she knew Bender could have placed a wire on him somewhere I an effort to gain a confession before they took her in. Knowing that he would continue, she didn't say a word.

"So if I don't want to see you go to jail, and then what am I going to do is what you're probably thinking" he said with a sinister grin. "Well here's the deal agent, today's your lucky day you only have to do two things for me and I'm going to let you completely off the hook young lady," he paused for a moment for a response, again she gave him none and he continued.

"The two things I'm going to need from you are fifty thousand dollars cash and your resignation from the bureau by tomorrow morning. I don't have to explain the outcome to you if don't do as I'm requesting here. It's going to read something like this, "Undercover FBI agent was indicted today on charges that she'd broken the bureaus code of ethics and began having relations as well as supplying case information to a suspected pimp that she'd been assigned to investigate." He paused for a moment to let it sink in before proceeding. "That's how the story will read on the front page of newsstands all across America. Now with that being said you have until 7am tomorrow to do both, I'm sure your new boyfriend won't have an issue giving you the money. Just to be sure to tell him that I'm going to see to it that the both of you get life behind bars if you fail to meet these demands," he said before rising up out the seat and walking away.

After he walked, away Chan sat there for a second cursing herself not for crossing the line with Keyshawn, but for being so careless and allowing Daley to compile so much dirt on her in such a short amount of time. She pondered his proposal it was highly unlikely that Bender was behind it the bureau didn't operate in that fashion – had they been behind it she would have gotten booked once they seen that Daley couldn't get her to talk. He was being greedy she was sure of it, and his greed was fueled by a mixture of jealousy and hate. Nevertheless, she was comfortable knowing that he hadn't revealed her wrongdoings to anyone else. The only question now was how exactly she would deal with the threat that he had posed.

Chapter Thirteen

The U.S. Courthouse & Federal Office Building in Milwaukee is a courthouse for the United States District Court for the Eastern District of Wisconsin. Built in 1892, the 115-year-old landmark's main public entrance was positioned on East Wisconsin Avenue in the downtown district of the city. The structure serves many facets of the U.S. government, from a post office to Senator's offices. But its main function is federal court proceedings, which could be accessed from a massive rotunda located just feet from the entry way.

The rear of the building located on Michigan Avenue was where the probation office and holding tanks were. After landing at Mitchell International Airport, the girls were driven straight there and after reading them their Miranda Rights agents along with prosecutors immediately began interrogation. The five women were placed in separate rooms equipped with audio/video recording features. This was common practice due to prisoners' manufacturing and discussing defense strategies with one another. The U.S. Attorney had one hour to be ready and he took full advantage once they arrived. The first one he approached with his presentation was Classy for no particular reason other than the fact that she occupied the first room in the hallway; from there he figured he would go on down the line.

Prosecutor O'Malley dressed in a navy blue suit and black Giorgio Armani loafers entered the room to find Classy balled-up on the chair with her hands tucked inside her shirt attempting to preserve the heat. The temperature was set lower in the interrogation rooms purposely so that detainees could be as uncomfortable as possible through past studies the C.I.A. had discovered that once an inmate became comfortable the chances of getting them to talk were even less at that point. So they adopted this method freezing suspects which was commonly known among its members as 'the freeze box treatment' An idea that became successful and was soon pasted down and followed by the F.B.I. then eventually local law enforcement agencies throughout the country.

"Hello Crystal, as I'm sure you know now I work for the United States government and it seems that you've fallen on our radar for some reason. Would you happen to know why?" he said taking a seat across from her.

Classy looked up at O'Malley; who was taking a seat; and started to stress her concerns for the conditions of the manner in which she was being housed.

"All I know is y'all need to turn the fucking heat up in this room, a bitch will freeze to death messing around in this muthafucka shit," she said tucking her head back between her legs.

"I'm sorry about that, but it's always cold in this place I don't know why they have the temperature set so low," he said lying. O'Malley's entire objective at this point was to appear to her as a friend, someone who could provide her with answers and a way to escape the trouble she was facing. He looked at her again before reaching into his briefcase, she still didn't respond.

"I don't think you and your friends know just how much trouble you're all in here, silence isn't gonna get you anywhere but on a plane to the USP female section of Hazelton out in West Virginia. Look, I am gonna get straight to the point and not play any games here okay. Your government has several felonies that we are prepared to seek indictments on and if you do not choose to cooperate here today, I can assure you that we will get them and you will be in prison for a long time. So first let's start with these," he said placing still photos from a surveillance tape of her at a jewelry store in Chicago purchasing a seventeen thousand dollar diamond chain with a stolen credit card. Keyshawn and T.A. had a relationship with a Russian jeweler there whom Red turned them onto and they would send the girls there to buy, sell, and trade merchandise when need be. There was no doubt it was her, Classy could remember that day from the pictures as if it were yesterday. She had met a trick at Arnie's in Harvey, IL and clipped him on a date for the card at the hotel room. At this point, however there was nothing she could do but stand up like a trooper.

"So you're showing me these pictures why again?" she said in a sarcastic tone.

O'Malley had been assigned to this case because he held the best conviction rate in the Eastern District when it came to human trafficking. So by no means was he a stranger to the depths of loyalty in the world of pimps and hoes. This was usually the position they took the task of getting one of them to debrief was equivalent to a person attempting a run a hundred yard dash in two seconds it was virtually impossible. But being the hard nose that he was O'Malley dug in deeper.

"As I've said Crystal that's not the only incriminating evidence we have against you. But just so you know that how serious I am I'm going to show you our ace in the whole," he said before opening up the door and stepping in the hallway briefly.

When he returned O'Malley was wearing the grin of a six-time NBA finals champion. Trailing directly behind him sporting a totally different demeanor was Special Agent Li Chan.

"You do remember Kimmie right Crystal? Well ya' see Kimmie isn't really who you guys thought she was, she's actually what we call a 'special agent' employed by the FBI and her job was to take you and your cronies down," he said pointing to the badge attached to the silver balled chain around Chan's neck.

"You look nice in a suit Kimmie not really my type of attire though," she said looking at Chan then back to O'Malley.

"Crystal this isn't a game you're going to jail for a very long time if you don't cooperate with us, you know that right?" Chan said. By now, all of Keyshawn's girls were aware of Chan's true identity, it was a decision he made to tell them knowing that it would bring them comfort during interrogation, thus lessening the chances of a debriefing. Classy played along.

"So what are you asking me to do?" she said looking dumbfounded. The prosecutor suddenly seen what he thought was a glimmer of hope.

"It's simple Crystal, you tell us all that you know about Keyshawn and T.A.'s activities and you walk scot free. We will first need you to testify in a secret hearing today and if they choose to go to trial which it highly doubtful; then we may need you to get on the stand a repeat what you'll say today." O'Malley knew from experience that once you have made your point it wasn't in the prosecutor's best interest to reiterate. He and Chan stared at Classy without anyone in the room blinking until she spoke.

"No thank you, and if I'm being charged with something at this time I would like a lawyer," she said reciting the script just as Chan had prepared it. Requesting a lawyer meant that he'd lost this battle and unless he wanted to lose the war - according to the law he had to immediately stop questioning and move on to the next cell. For that O'Malley was heated now, he couldn't believe his ace in the hole trick was a bust. Leaving he shared his final words.

"There are a thousand others like you and you wanna know where they are, in max joints doing twenty-five and up. You've gotta be out of your mind protecting this guy, you actually think he gives a shit about you?" he said shaking his head. Classy was a rock and he knew it, which was more of a reason for him to hang Key and T.A. up on hooks. Her honor to the game not only strengthened his cause but it was fuel to his Adam Walsh way of thinking.

"I understand, but like I said I want a lawyer" Classy expressed one last time before they both promptly left the room.

Following a quick do's and don'ts session they had in the hallway before heading in to interrogate Venus was a message from his assistant Patrick notifying O'Malley that the girls all had lawyers presently waiting in their office requesting to see their clients. His fears had become reality, and with regards to his game plan for the day O'Malley was now 0 for 2. After glancing at his watch, he ordered Patrick to fetch the lawyers along with agents Daley and Smith to assist them. There was only forty minutes left before the hearing and he wanted to make they were able to have some sort of a lunch beforehand.

Seth Bennis had no idea why he was called to a meeting in the fourth floor conference room. There was no need for him to be on the floor especially when it evolved Sidney Bender. In his entire eight-year tenure with the bureau, he had been there a total of three times. Hearing about a few promotions that were underway in the elevator he toyed with the idea of landing one of them himself today.

Upon exiting the elevator, he walked down the hall a short way to the room where he had been ordered to be. There he found Bender alone by himself with the door open.

"Please come in and close agent," he said leaning back in the chair. Seth did as he was told and took a seat.

"I want to start by saying that I've always thought that you were a brilliant and fine agent." Those words gave him the assurance that he needed, it was official he was about to gain a promotion!

"But we have a problem and it seems the only clue we have here is one that leads to you," Bender said studying Bennis.

"Problem, sir what sort of problem," Seth said completely confused now.

"Several hundred hours of wire-tap files along with back-ups have been deleted from our systems central hard drive, would you happen to know anything about that agent?" Just then agent Edith Philips from the Electronic Communications department and Matthew Riley from Internal Investigations opened the door and walked.

Seth was stunned by what he was hearing he wasn't sure if he was being accused of being the culprit who deleted the files or simply if they were just asking around the bureau. Until he answered his own question, the F.B.I. didn't just ask questions for the sake of wonder. If they approached you in that manner, something is pushing them to believe you have the answer to their question.

"I, I don't understand sir why would I know something about what?" he was stumbling over his thoughts now. Riley sensed his nervousness and looked at Bender who gave him the okay, then he went full speed ahead.

"Agent our records are showing that your username and password was the ones used in order to conduct these actions. Is there any way you can explain that to us please?" he said hoping that Seth could provide them with some sort of reasonable explanation.

Seth was dumbfounded at this point missing wire-taps with the finger pointing towards him! This had to be a mistake. He realized the seriousness of the allegations and felt obligated to defend himself.

"No of course not! I've never deleted any files and surely not any wire-taps. That's not even my department, why would I be looking to do that," he said in his defense.

"Well do you know how this possibly could have happened; could someone possibly have gotten a hold to your username and password?" Matthew Riley said.

"I have no idea, umm I don't, and I've never given anyone my password. This has to be some sort of mix-up," he said hoping it was. Bender sat up in his seat.

"We understand agent, however at this time I have no choice but to temporarily relieve you of your duties pending an investigation into these matters. You understand that this is a serious matter the bureau doesn't take this sort of thing lightly. There was very important information in regards to a case we are now working to close agent Bennis."

"I'm sure it was sir, but I didn't delete files," Seth even more nervous now.

"I see, well agent there will be some people here to escort you to your desk to gather whatever you'd like to take home after that you are not enter the premises without prior approval from my or I.I. office. We'll be in touch," Bender said before they all rose from the table and left the room. Within minutes, two security agents were there to take him where he needed to be.

Chapter Fourteen

While the government prepared to bring them to their knees, Keyshawn and T.A. were busy countering their moves at hotel café just blocks from the courthouse. Immediately following their arrests, the pair summoned legal representation to the federal building to act as their mouths, eyes, and ears. As they sat in a corner placing and receiving calls from the attorneys an agent was at a table alone pretending to be reading a Field & Streams magazine. Neither of them noticed him nor did they care, as advised by the attorneys they were both within legal parameters of the law therefore at this point couldn't be arrested for any reason without an indictment.

What they now knew was that the lawyers had contact with the girls and they were in discussions with the prosecutor's office their detainment without due process in other words proper subpoena.

~ ❖ ~

Attorneys Harry Levitt and Nigel Brunswick were senior partners in the law firm Levitt, Brunswick, & Nelson. Their arrival brought swiftness to the interviews the outcome was the same in each room, as they had all refused to answer any questions and referred the examiner to their counselors. While the attorneys were at work, their associates were in the Clerk of Courts office filing petitions requesting the court to grant injunction relief for unlawful seizure of the women. Upon review of the subpoena's they were arguing that the United States had not served the detainees subpoenas in a proper time frame, therefore not granting them adequate time to appear, thus making their arrests illegal. Temporary Injunctions were ordered by a magistrate, the order as read was to the women in custody and to defer the grand jury's hearing until he could decide on the petition. It was a diminutive victory for the lawyers; however, the postponement would give them a few more hours to prep their clients before the inquisition.

Counsel from both sides was in court prepared to argue their case before U. S. Magistrate Anthony Gaines. As the lawyers and detainees filed in to take their seats, Gaines was exiting chambers. Once the bailiff finished his spill and everyone were seated they began.

"This matter is in regards to a petition filed by the detainees counsel concerning the arrest and detention of the five women before us," Gaines said looking over his wire-rimmed glasses at the audience.

"It seems that counsel believes that their clients are being held by our government illegally, am I correct gentleman?"

"Yes, that is correct your honor," both lawyers said in unison.

"Very well, we'll hear from the governments counsel first," the short stubby Magistrate, said sinking into the gigantic black leather chair. O'Malley sprang into action immediately.

"Your honor, the government has been investigating a case against the men of these detainees for some time now. Men who we know to be not only violent people, manipulative as well. It is our position that if these women were to be released there's a strong possibility that certain evidence; which they can provide to our case will be greatly compromised. It would be an unduly act justice for the court to allow such a thing. In the Bail Reform Act of 1984: 18 U.S.C. 3144 the law clearly states that any person whom has information that is alleged to be *material* concerning a criminal proceeding are then therefore a "material witness" and the government has the power and authority to arrest and detain that person if the court so feels that lost or tampering of evidence was a threat to the overall case. So your honor, the government thinks that that threat exists and there is a great chance that it will happen if in fact these women were released without allowing us to bring them before a grand jury beforehand." When

O'Malley seen that the Magistrate appeared to be pondering his words he stopped to gauge him further. Any good lawyer knew that half of the game in court was body language when arguing a point, too much or too little could make or break you.

The opposing counsels contemplating what he'd said as well. None of which was a surprise, the only legs the government had to stand on was the Bail Reform Act of 1984. Both lawyers were considering additional rebuttals as the magistrate began to speak.

"The court will now hear from Mr. Levitt and Mr. Brunswick," he said without providing a hint as to what he was thinking. Gaines had a reputation at the courthouse for being fair, yet difficult to read. There wasn't an attorney who didn't like him, the fact that he couldn't be read was a gift to both the plaintiff and defense so neither had a grievance in that area. Levitt was standing to begin.

"Your honor what the prosecutor is attempting to do by locking these women up without bail is an act of kidnapping. These young women weren't properly served with a subpoena before they were arrested and dragged in to testify for the government. In U.S. versus Carignan, 342: 36 the law clearly states that no one can be imprisoned without due process. In this case our clients were denied due process; simply because the prosecutors didn't follow proper procedures furnishing them with subpoenas to appear before the grand jury prior to assuming that they would not show or that somehow their testimony would have been damaged or tainted had they been 'giving the heads up', he said looking at O'Malley in disgust.

"This is completely unlawful and a disgrace to the fair legal system that we have established here in this country. So therefore your honor we will argue that our clients be immediately released and allowed to attend these hearings through their own free will, which I will assure the court that they will do." When Levitt sat down his partner leaned in to offer encouragement.

"You did well buddy," he said quickly before returning to his position to hear what the Gaines would say next.

Anytime he gave an opening argument Levitt would be sweating by the armpits; it was a phobia that he hadn't exposed to anyone except Brunswick. He'd been practicing law for nearly a decade and still got the tremors when opening up. But following a drink of water he'd always be fine.

Following a brief recess Gaines was ready to make his ruling. Before speaking, he skimmed through a small stack of papers then glanced at both sides momentarily.

"In considering the matter before this court I've had several facts to consider all of which were legitimate arguments made by both counsels here today," he said looking at Levitt and O'Malley again. Both Brunswick and Levitt weren't too sure in a victory, although their argument held merit it was still a longshot based on the overall circumstances of their client's detainment. Patrick O'Malley felt as though he had been operating within the confines of the law therefore was confident the ruling would be in the governments favor.

"The government raised the issue of witness and evidence tampering, while the petitioners are arguing lack of due process and false imprisonment. In reference back to the point Mr. Levitt made in regards to U.S. vs. Carignan I have found that the petitioner was indeed not served proper subpoena by the government, but has not been imprisoned improperly nor are they being held unlawful. Therefore, not to depreciate order and the law I have no other choice but to rule in favor of the government. The petitioners shall remain in custody without bail until a proceeding of the grand jury is concluded," he said before striking the mallet.

"What does that mean, how long we have to stay in here," Venus said not completely understanding the ruling.

"It means they are holding you all until the prosecutor has his indictment hearing," Brunswick said in a sober voice. Sure, he figured they would lose the ruling, but thought that a proper balance of justice would have included the magistrate granting them a bail with certain restrictions of contact towards T.A. and Keyshawn.

Chapter Fifteen

Michelle was at the grocery store when she received the call on her cell phone. It was from the St. Mary's hospital.

"Ms. Watson, this is Nurse Vivian Landry at St. Mary's lakeshore hospital, and I'm calling you in regards to Timothy." When she heard that Michelle was immediately relieved, there wasn't a day that went by that she hadn't dreaded getting a call about something unfortunate happening to Keyshawn.

"No ma'am I wish I could say he was but he isn't. Timothy was checked in to our I.C.U. today around an hour ago. He's not doing well at all I take it that you are aware of his situation?" she said with caution.

"Yes, he told me and the kids a few weeks ago about his cancer."

"Okay, well I suggest that you all come and see him immediately Ms. Watson," she said lowering her voice to a more saddened tone. Michelle understood where the nurse was headed but she simply didn't want to hear anymore.

"Okay, we'll be there and thank you very much for calling me Ms. Landry."

"Not a problem," she said before they both hung up.

~ ❖ ~

Keysha was at Marquette's registrations office switching a few classes around on her schedule when she received the call.

"Hey ma' what's going on?" she said stepping into the hallway.

"Hey baby, what you up to?" she said stalling with the news, Michelle didn't like to see her daughter's spirits down and she knew this would hurt her.

"At school handling a few things, is everything okay you sound a little weird right now mama?" Keysha said, sensing the worry in her mother's tone. Her first thought went to Keyshawn and T.A.'s situation.

"I got a call from, St. Mary's baby, your fathers in there and they say he's not doing well, the nurse urged me to come and see him. I wanted you and your brother to come with me and see about him in a little bit Pooh." Michelle rarely called Keysha by that name, and when she did, it was usually during consoling.

Keysha had prepared for this day ever since their dad had informed them of his condition. She didn't want to be hurt any more than she already was. So to protect herself she would say things like, "he's dead or there's nothing we can do he's gonna die soon" and so far it helped with the pain.

"Alright ma', I'll be leaving here shortly just call me when you're ready."

"Are you gone be okay baby girl," Michelle said.

"Yeah ma' I'm fine, don't start this okay." Keysha didn't want her mom to bring up feelings that she was doing her best to hold down. She knew Michelle was just being a concerned mother to her only daughter, but at times, it only made matters worse.

"Alright, I'll see you soon."

After clearing the line, she attempted Keyshawn three times before he answered. When he finally did he responded by saying, "Okay, I'll try and make it out there later." Michelle understood and respected his position he was free to handle the situation however, he chose.

Here he was with his life and future on the line, and somehow he was supposed to find sympathy and compassion for a man who never gave too shits about him or his family. Tim's health and well-being was the furthest thing from his mind; in fact, he could actually give a fuck if he lived or died.

At 3 p.m. and the hearing was starting well behind schedule. Prosecutor O'Malley strolled into the closed courtroom alone with the same air of confidence that he displayed each time he starred in one of these lopsided inquiries. As he situating evidence on the large bench, he cursed the FB.I. for not securing him with the wire-taps, and as he attempted to understand what could have possibly happened to them the Marshals were escorting his audience inside to perform their civic duties. Once the sixteen members were completely filed in, the door was locked and the three marshals stood outside on guard.

In accordance with the Federal Rules of Criminal Procedure all proceedings and statements made before a Grand Jury are sealed, meaning that only the people in the room have knowledge about who said what about whom. No one, (not even a judge) is permitted to attend these deliberations except the U.S. Attorney and the jurors. Witnesses may be compelled to testify in order to weight their testimony towards the prosecutors' outline of the case. The body (jury) is a constitutional requirement that exists so that a group of citizens, who do not know the defendant, the judge, the prosecutor or anyone else in the room, can make an unbiased decision as to the existence of enough evidence to charge a defendant with a crime.

As O'Malley walked around the table nearest to them, he leaned back against it in comfort, and then began his show.

"This case is pretty simple folks the F.B.I. began investigating a man by the name of Keyshawn

Watson after they received word from New Orleans that a prostitute who was brought there by him had been murdered by whom we later found was a rival pimp. F.B.I. was able to make contact with Watson early on and was able to infiltrate his organization with a female agent at the bureau. During their investigation, they discovered two more people whom he conspired with; T.A. Smith and another man Devin Highshaw, who is now deceased. We are seeking indictments on charges of Conspiracy to Sex Traffic, Bribery of a Public Official, and Money Laundering. I have a host of witnesses including an agent with the F.B.I. that will further prove their involvement in these crimes along with documentation of property purchased by these individuals through illicit means, as well as video surveillance footage. At this time I will bring in Agent Li Chan as my first witness," he said walking over to the door to secure the marshal.

Li Chan entered the room and made her way to the witness stand. There was something different about her the prosecutor noticed, she appeared tired. O'Malley approached the witness stand.

"Agent can you please state your full name and job title for grand jury please," he said preparing to have her take the oath. Standing directly in front of her he could see that her face was damp and Chan looked as though she was sweating.

"Yes, my name is Li Chan and I work for the United States Federal Bureau of Investigations," she said.

"Thank you, now will you please stand and place your right hand on the bible for me." She did as directed with no comment. Once erect Chan was swaying to the point of where she had to utilize the rail of the witness booth to hold herself up.

"Do you swear to tell the whole truth and nothing but the truth so help you God?" O'Malley asked her looking into Chan's eye.

"Yes, I"... There was a long pause as she struggled to gather herself to finish. Anticipating a collapse O'Malley closed in on her.

"Agent are you okay?" he said placing his hand upon her upper back. She responded in a feeble tone.

"Yeah, um I'm fine," she said. But he wasn't convinced.

"Come let me assist you to the door." Upon transport of Chan to the marshal he asked him to locate Agent Daley and for Crystal (Classy) Milton to be sent in, then walked back to his table.

In the mist of reorganizing his itinerary, O'Malley felt the energy of the panel lying upon him. Stopping briefly, he rose up to address them.

"Folks I'm sorry for the delay, as you've seen our witness wasn't feeling well. We will be moving along here momentarily. Just as he finished the door was opened and Classy cross its threshold but abruptly stopped a few steps from the entrance.

"Ms. Milton please come this way and have a seat at the witness stand," O'Malley said pointing to her destination.

Classy was gravely irritated by now she had been through two airports, two different jails, three holding cells, and now two court appearances all on one meal. Her walk to the podium conveyed that to the room.

O'Malley wasn't at all impressed with the vibe he was acquiring from his witness. He sensed trouble, but figured he had nothing to lose if she failed to cooperate it would not be the dead of his case. He proceeded to the bench, and following the oath, he began.

"Ms. Milton I'm going to ask you some questions in regards to your relationship with Keyshawn Watson. But before we begin I would like to reiterate that you are not on trial here nor is this a trial." Classy kneeled down to adjust the tongue on her Christian Dior sneakers, the laces were taken away from her upon entry into the holding facility in Milwaukee. When she rose back up O'Malley was about to repeat himself but instead continued on.

"Can you please tell me the relationship between yourself and Mr. Watson?"

"I plead the fifth," she said.

"Okay, well how long have you known Keyshawn Watson?" O'Malley said hoping that he could get her to engage in the conversation some sort of way. Classy wasn't about to hear of it, she'd been coached well.

"I plead the fifth," she said with folded arms and curled her lips.

At that point O'Malley understood where this was going he excused her from the stand and called on Venus who repeated the exact same ritual. It was as if they had practiced this routine. Following her testimony he went through the entire witness list receiving the same results until a former disgruntled hooker of T.A.'s by the name of Natalie Westbrook was called upon. She concurred with the prosecutor when asked if T.A. was indeed a pimp, she went on to give graphic details of times that she'd been beaten and witnessed other women in his stable get beaten to the point of passing out. Her testimony was by far the most damaging of any the jury had heard. Then after she was finished, O'Malley followed up with Agent Daley who blew the case out of the water. Once it was wrapped up and handed to the grand jury for a decision, they were out for approximately fourth-five minutes before returning with indictments on Keyshawn and T.A. on all counts. O'Malley was elated although he was certain from the very beginning of what he believed the outcome would be it still gave him great pride to know that justice (in his mind) was being served.

Chapter Sixteen

The air was crisp on that autumn evening; as the pair cruised through the town in Keyshawn's Benz, Remy, and Dro were the order of the evening. Although they were both thoroughly convinced that the grand jury would indict prior to the ruling hearing the news still had its impact. Mutually they began to prepare themselves for the possibilities of federal prison had things not went so well with their Kimmie's plan.

"So what you think about this mess lil homie?" T.A. said pondering the conversation; they had had with the attorneys following the decision.

"I'm not sure; we don't know the details yet T. I just wanna know what charges they about to try and stick on us mane. I'm getting a full report from Kimmie later on tonight," he said navigating through traffic.

"This some cold shit mane, these fags tryna' put a nigga away for pimping! This whole fucking country was founded on illicit activities Key. But now sense these pussies done established their land; that they stole mind you; they wanna come with the regulation game on niggas who looking to make their mark on the world pure bullshit playboy!" T.A. was speaking from his philosophy of the way he believed society should be run. Leaders and men who believed that the only rules that existed were the one whom an individual founded themselves raised him.

"I feel you that's, why I'm not going down without a fight," Keyshawn said hitting the blunt before passing it.

"I mean the way they coming at us, you would think that we was fucking with some kids or some shit man. Out of all the shit that's going on around here, they wanna target pimps for simply creating a way out of a fucked up situation" he said looking at Keyshawn as if he was asking a question.

"I mean since when does a nigga get punished for being a better thinker than busters and lames homie! They rather see us living in the ghetto with pipes in our mouths' cause that's the way they designed the outcome. Every last one of those bitches is grown and did everything they did by choice pimp. So you tell me what the fucks wrong with this picture?!" Keyshawn wasn't saying a word; he just listened and processed the information as he'd always done when game was being handed down.

After a finishing the blunt and hitting a few more corners they decided to stop at "The Underground", a night club on the east side of town that one of T.A.'s uncles owned. When they pulled up Bone's black Lexus was parked near the front entrance alongside the vehicles of various family members who regularly frequented the joint.

The door was locked and guarded by none other than Clay-Jack a big black brother from Mississippi whom been with the family since the earlier days when the elders were still heavily active in the life.

"What's up nephews? Y'all came down here to win some of this money too?" he said referring to the dice game that was underway on top of the pool table. Clay-Jack referred to the entire younger generation of the unit simply as "nephew" just as most of the old-heads did who'd seen them grow-up over the years.

"What's going down CJ? These dudes gambling huh, is unc. in here?" T.A. said scanning the place swiftly before spotting Big Daddy.

"Yea he over there cutting the game, you know that nigga ain't about to miss no money. Y'all go on in, and T. make sure you holla' at me before you leave I got some news you can use." He said patting him on the back as they cruised through the threshold.

Donnell Jones was harmonizing from the jukebox about *Where he wanted to be* as they made their way past the front bar, there was a table of attractive young women sitting across from it right next to the poker machine that were whispering to one another while thirsting for a hustler's attention. Keyshawn glanced their way momentarily, recognizing one of the girls from his old middle school. She waved at him with an arm and lustful eyes of approval in a desperate attempt to lure him towards their area.

"I ain't got time for them hoes," he thought to himself when he caught her rubbernecking. His lack of interest did a number on the longhaired caramel skinned beauty.

"Girl, niggas kill me with that funny acting shit when they get a lil money. I remember when he was selling them skimpy ass bags of weed just a few years ago," she said rolling her eyes. Varasia wasn't use to rejection rarely did she go out of her way to pursue a man, and each time that she had the outcome was just as she'd projected. But Keyshawn was cut from an extraordinary cloth, one that viewed good looks simply as a tool to obtaining riches. His response had been calculated, and worked just as it always did.

"Tuh, anyway Robyn call them dudes we met at Millennium last night and tell 'em to meet us down here," she said in an effort to repair what damage he had conducted on her self-image and ego. "Two real PIMPS done fell up in here" Big Daddy yelled out as they were arriving to the make shift crap table. Bone looked up and over his shoulder to see whom his uncle was referring to.

"What's happenin' unc?" T.A. said with a smile, it was always a treat for him to be in the company of Big Daddy, he appreciated his energy.

"What's going down P's?" Bone said shaking their hands.

"Nothing much are you winning," Keyshawn responded.

"Yea just a couple dollars, you know this isn't really my kind of gamble, I'm just fucking off 'til' later," Bone said in reiteration to the fact that he wasn't allowed to play his way do to it being a friendly clean game amongst kin and friends.

"I feel you, let me get in on some of this action though," Keyshawn said squeezing between Bone and Mitch, which was another longtime associate of the family. T.A. went around to the other side where there was additional room.

An older gentleman by the name of Willy had control of the dice at the moment, and each time he rolled looking for his point he'd stop afterwards to ask that the dice be mixed up before he continued on with his next roll.

"Say Willy, now you know there's supposed to be a cut every time you want a shake up? I been letting you past, but you just can't keep doing that expecting not to pay," Big daddy said in a diplomatic tone. Known for his fairness, he was always skilled with the ability of bringing crowds of people from all walks of the street life together in any room without incident.

"Well long as I owe you, you'll never be broke," he said jokingly before firing out the dice down the table towards the opposite end.

"Naw, long as you keep rolling dem dice I'ma get my cut, you old muthafucka," Big Daddy said laughing but serious. Willy along with a few other players couldn't resist the hilarity.

"Yeah, whatever nigga just give me another shake-up," he said causing the entire table to break out laughing in amusement. Everyone knew that he and Big Daddy had a mutual respect for one another that allowed them to crack jokes and make fun, but never any maliciousness.

When they landed, the cubes registered seven.

"Alright you old muthafucka' pass the dice and wait for your next turn," he said snickering. As the players were collecting their winnings and the next shooter prepared to strike, Big Daddy directed his attention to T.A., who was now standing next to him.

"You know that lil chick over there in the red be getting some good money mane, one of y'all might wanna go holla' before she leave here tonight," he said to T.A. referring to one of the girls who would come there with Key's old friend Varasia.

"Yeah, I saw them. I am straight though unc. I'm not even feeling those bitches right now." A response that was completely out of character for T.A., Big

Daddy had never known him to turn down his collar when it came to the possibility of knocking off a new prospect.

"What's going on nephew? You alright, it ain't like you to pass up on some action pimp?"

"Yeah, I'm good unc, just got a few things on my mind that's all. You know them people brought back indictments on me and the homie today?" he whispered near his ear while gesturing towards Keyshawn. Big Daddy was taken away by the news.

"What! how this happen?" he said completely focused on his nephew at this point. T.A. didn't want any extra ears hearing their conversation.

"Let's step over here real quick."

"Okay, aye Fred cover the game for a second," Big Daddy said to a friend as he pushed back from the pool table. Everyone called him Big Daddy because he was the eldest of the Smith clan that was living. T.A. regularly sought counsel through him due to his uncles' rich supply of knowledge.

Walking over to the bar, Big Daddy took a few orders from patrons who wanted their drinks replenished. Although he had a crew of bartenders, he had always preferred to be hands on when it came to his business.

After satisfying the customers, he poured a double shot of cognac for his young nephew.

"So what's the deal here youngin' how'd they jam you mane?" he said taking a seat across from T.A. on the backside of the bar.

"It's a long story unc., but in a nut shell the bullshit all stemmed from that bitch move the nigga Smoove pulled on lil homie in N.O.," he said in an aggravating tone before taking a swig of the expensive fluid. Big Daddy was searching his memory to find what situation T.A was referring to in regards to Smoove.

"Oh, you talking about that thing with the girl. You know I never pegged dude to be that kind of nigga mane, I mean since when do Players perform sucka stunts like that!" he said shaking his head. "The worst trick a pimp can ever play on himself is to believe that a hoe is a lifetime possession, they change pimps like money change hands mane, and don't belong to nobody but the game." As most players who heard of Smoove's short-coming, Big Daddy was at a complete loss to that situation. But from time to time the streets would tell a story of a player who'd badly fumbled and tricked off his life in the process, and that the O.G. was no stranger to.

"Yeah that's the same shit I said. But dig they put a fed bitch along with a few others in our business and the fags been on us ever since unc... We haven't been saying shit because key was able to flip the chick and now we got the broad in our pocket. She a few months pregnant by lil dawg and we got all kinds of additional dirt on her that I was thinking may have kept us out here, but with this punk shit they jumped off today I'm not so sure."

"Wow, you cats are in some deep waters. I'm not sure what all you have on the girl, but whatever it is it still may not secure a victory for you dudes. You do know that right?" he said before pausing. Just then, Keyshawn walked up.

"What's happenin'? I know y'all chopping up some super-fly shit over here," he said playing with the money he had won in the crap game.

"Always my man always, what you drinking?" Big Daddy said reaching for a glass.

"Remy unc.."

"Yeah, but that's what I was saying unc, what good will it actually do if we expose her hand?" T.A. said responding to the question that was posed prior to Keyshawn joining them.

"It may do you no good at all, in fact it may backfire and actually work against y'all, and if the wrong judge gets a hold to that case he may view her as just another victim whose been trapped and manipulated into the web of a gamer."

"You really think they'd go that far?" Keyshawn interjected after bringing himself up to speed.

"Do I? Nephew I don't put nothing past them folks. Don't get me wrong now, if it comes out that the bitch has been supplying y'all with information she's fucked - they're gonna nail her ass to the cross. But for them having to sacrifice one of their own, oh the penalties for you and Key will be five times worst. They will put it out there to the public like y'all influenced a naïve person that wasn't equipped to fight off the game of a pimp. Although we both know it's some complete garbage, we live in a world where the vast majority of folks believe what they hear, especially when they're not from the hood and the information's coming from a reputable source such as a fucking D.A.! Oh and you can bet your bottom dollar that the jury will be a bunch of out of towners who are off of touch with the real world and how it operates, thus leading to a fast conviction if y'all go to trial." They were listening to wisdom, and the truth couldn't be ignored.

"That's some straight up bullshit unc," T.A. said with an expression of disgust.

"Tell me about it, but with the language they have written into federal laws, it makes cases nearly impossible to beat that's why they have a fucking ninety-eight percent conviction rate, and out of that ninety-eight sixty percent of them take pleas," he said tossing his hands in the air.

"So in other words you're saying that this ace in the hole we thought we had actually doesn't hold any weight at all?" Keyshawn said not fully prepared to write off Li Chan as being their sacrificial lamb just yet.

"No I'm not saying that, the element of surprise always has its advantages baby boy. So by exposing her hand you can rest fasho' that it's gonna have 'em scrambling, and in turn there's a strong possibility that it may cause this U.S. attorney to come with a really sweet deal simply because the powers that be may not want to air their dirty laundry. Nephew you gotta understand these people are extremely big on preserving this false image of law enforcement that they portray to the public. But the flip side to that coin is by throwing her under the bus you'd be corroborating their case and who knows at that point they might say "fuck her" and use your trump card to take everybody down." A look of nervousness and perplexity appeared on both their faces.

"They play the game dirty nephews, you two nigga's need to get together and collectively make a decision on how y'all tryna' see this play out. I will tell you one thing, this chick is stand-up people and if it was me in you cats situation I would have to lay on the knife if need be. She's more of an asset to a nigga in the position she's in not no fucking jail cell. You dudes young there's life after that shit if it goes sour," Big

Daddy said echoing the laws that had been passed down to them from day one.

Around midnight they received calls from the girls requesting to be picked up at federal holding in Waukesha. Once they were finished testifying the order from the Magistrate was for them to be released, but since they failed to cooperate with O'Malley, he acted as if their paperwork had been misplaced somehow. Then they mysteriously materialized at 7:30 a half an hour before he left his office to head home for the night.

When Keyshawn and T.A. received the call they were still slicing game with Big Daddy, but both abruptly left after hearing the good news. Following a quick nearby pit stop to retrieve T.A.'s Jag, Keyshawn trailed him on I-94 West to Waukesha County Jail.

Chapter Seven

To Keyshawn the twenty-five minute ride seemed more like an hour even as he waited in the parking lot of the jail for his team the anticipation of yearning to know what the special prosecutor had on his mind; had him restless and jittery.

Classy was the first to emerge, she appeared blaring obscenities to someone on the inside while walking backwards towards the concrete stairs.

"What the fuck is this girl doing?" he said to himself as he rolled down the window in an effort to make out her words. But the exchange was just as short as her hike had been to the car. When she reached the door her left hand and arm was occupied with personal property that was deemed unsafe by the jail staff.

"Hey, baby! I told them bitches my nigga would be out here front and center whenever they let me free," she said climbing into the Benz.

"Who was yo' crazy ass arguing with on the way out?" he said studying the contents in the plastic bag Classy placed in her lap.

"One of those punk ass deputies daddy his ole' bitch ass gone tell us we need to get some real jobs and stop destroying relationships."

"Don't pay chumps like that a never-mind baby he's just got his panties up his ass because you pull more money in a month than him and his fairytale bitches probably make in a whole year. Suckas like that the main ones creeping through the blade looking to score a quick fix of some pussy on their lunch break."

"You right daddy screw him. Oh, I just realized how much I missed you!" she said leaning over the seat to hug and kiss him on the cheek.

"Girl yo' butt act like you been in there forever," he said while laughing during their embrace.

"I know, but that's how I felt in there baby," she said rubbing her face up against his naked chin.

Having been in her shoes before, Keyshawn understood where she was coming from, being incarcerated for any amount of time had its way of making one appreciate the simple freedoms and blessings that life had to offer.

"Where's everybody else at?" he said looking at the entrance.

"I don't know, we were all in the same room right before they let me out." Just then, the others began filing out of the glass doors with T.A. hoe Angelica leading the way. The colorful scene resembled that of one from the movie *Willie Dynamite*, only minus the circus show.

Agent Smith watched nearby as the girls made their way to the vehicles and the two groups deserted the area heading for the city.

In route to their domain, Keyshawn received a call from him and Kimmie's buffer requesting him to meet her at their mom's house for a quick meeting. When he pulled up, she was sitting in the driveway talking to Brandon on a call from the House of Correction. As he was approaching the car, Keyshawn noticed that she wasn't attentive to his presence and decided to give his twin a lesson on 'hood alertness.' He tiptoed alongside the black Nissan Altima and snatched the door open. Keysha jerked towards the right, away from what she thought was danger.

"What the... Nigga you betta' stop playing," she said catching her breath.

"Naw, you need to take more interest in your surroundings, what I tell yo' ass about that? You ain't in Mayberry girl this ain't the Andy Griffin show," he said kneeling down beside her door.

"So what's going on, did she call?" he said referring to Kimmie.

"Yeah, she wants y'all to meet around 2 O'clock at "the spot in Fox Point," Keysha said with a question mark on her face.

"Okay."

"I assumed you knew where she was talking about."

"So she didn't say anything else huh?" he said glancing around the area.

"No, we didn't get into any details, when she said that I responded with "okay" and hung up."

"Good, at least you did something right today," he said jokingly.

"Haha, go da' hell, you let something happen to me and mama gone kill yo' ass," she said sticking her tongue out in defense.

"Whatever man, see you later."

"Alright, love you lil dude now close my door so I can finish talking to my boo in peace."

"You to take yo' ass in the house and how the hell y'all on the phone this late? Lights been out since 10pm," he said in curiosity.

"See that's just like a nigga to be all in the business, don't worry about it we stay plugged shawty," she said giggling. "Naw, but he got a cell phone bro. we really don't do the collect call thing."

"That's what's up! Tell homie I said to keep his head up and make his bed up, and you need to either leave or go in the house it's too late."

"Ain't nobody about to be out here, I about to leave okay dang," she said turning over the engine.

"A'ight' later," he said closing her door before trotting off to the Benz.

~ ~

Back at home while the girls showered one by one, T.A. didn't waste any time questioning them on what all was said at the hearing and by whom. After hearing that everybody had stuck with the plan, which was to plead the fifth, he commended them both on their steadfastness to him, the game, themselves, and more importantly the family. There wasn't anything said to him that he hadn't already expected O'Malley to have asked, except for the fact that Natalie Westbrook's name came up a few times during questioning. Since Angelica was the only one who knew "Natty," as they called her, he dug into her the deepest.

"So what all did he say about the Natty bitch baby?" he asked sinking his back into the posh Roche Bobis leather settee.

"It was the D.A. dude, he just asked me if I knew her and when I told him that I didn't he said that he knew I was lying because they had information from sources confirming that she was with you when we met." His wheels were turning now, and he figured that to be some bullshit on O'Malley's behalf, the source was Natty herself.

"Sources huh?" he said aloud. "I see and I'm sure he never revealed any of those so-called 'sources' right?" She shook her head no. T.A. understood the play, the government had Natty in their pocket to be used as a collaboration piece. But the question that boggled him was how they even knew about her? Natty had long since fled his pimping nearly a year before they began investigating him. She was a certified breadwinner, but couldn't control her jealousy. When Angelica chose-up she immediately became intimidated upon laying eyes on the young European stallion and started kicking up drama in T.A.'s camp. Prior to Angelica coming on board she had been with him for three calendars, in that time, Natty had contributed well over a half of a million dollars to the family. Figures that lead her to begin throwing ideas at T.A. about them retiring away from the other hoes and making another life somewhere else with kids, the white picket fence, and a dog. A picture that he knew was being painted in her head by the sense of entitlement that she had over the others. Not to mention one that he wasn't ready for, the young mack had yet to reach his prime and wasn't about to be deterred. He respected her desire to want what she did, but it wouldn't be with him. Hearing that Natty tried another approach, she actually came to him submitting the ridiculous request of her being allowed to retain half of her trap money. An idea that almost drove him to disrespecting the audacious whore, but he didn't, it wasn't an easy task but he kept his cool. To surrender to her demands would be a spit in the face to the game and his hoes, who were giving him their absolute all. So instead of falling for the okey doke, T.A. did her one better. He sent her on a booking to an established whore house for a month gave her twenty-five hundred dollars, bought her plane ticket, and told her that she was no longer apart of the stable and gave her his blessings in her life journeys.

Instead of pushing her away, his diplomacy did nothing but magnify the desire of her wanting to be with him. After being gone for a week she regretted she had ever toyed with the idea she proposed to him, and in turn began calling him pleading to have her place back at home, but he denied her request. She attempted to call with the sentimental game speaking of the years and time they had been together, but again her pleas were to no avail. This drove her to a spiteful form of resentment and anger towards him, and when she returned home to Milwaukee five weeks, later the emotionally scarred woman kicked off a vicious campaign to sabotage T.A.'s life as well as his pimp career. From spreading propaganda in phone calls to his current whores to calling the property management company at his previous place of residence, she put in overtime towards seeing her plan through. It wasn't until the girls spotted her in a local nail salon getting a fill, and beat her all but to a coma did she cease her malicious acts.

Although there weren't any overt actions being shown, T.A. was game savvy enough to know that the level of hatefulness she displayed for him wasn't something that disappeared with an ass whooping, he believed that she was simply waiting on the precise time to execute her best move.

He couldn't have been more right, Natty had been approached by the feds when Agent Smith was investigating T.A's arrest record in Milwaukee. Documents showed that two years prior she had been a passenger in a vehicle he was operating, at which time he had been detained for a child support paternity test warrant. Smith further discovered that a three thousand dollar bail had been posted for T.A. in Natty's name around the same time. Upon investigating, he quickly found that Natty did in fact have one arrest for prostitution in the city of Las Vegas almost six months after she had bailed T.A. out of jail in Milwaukee. The room that he was busted in was registered to an Angelica Van Plaus. Once it was established that she'd been affiliated with the ring at one point Agent Smith set out to track Natalie Westbrook down in an effort to obtain any helpful information that she could give them on the him and his cronies. To his surprise, Natalie was more than willing to debrief and cooperate with the investigation.

"This actually doesn't surprise me," T.A. said to Angelica as Autumn came into the area from her bath to join them. "Her testimony wasn't the deciding factor in them scoring the indictment, it was just another piece to the puzzle that was gone get placed together with or without that funky backstabbing bitch." Angelica was pissed.

"Daddy, I never liked that bitch, I always knew she wasn't any good, the slut has done nothing but caused trouble since I've been here. I mean come on now, what kind of hoe goes to these extremes though. We shoulda' killed her punk ass that day," Angelica said.

"Either that or kicked the bitch's voice box out with a steel-toe boot shit," Autumn said looking at her wife-in-law.

"I know right, that wouldn't have been a bad idea girl, I can't stand a fuckin' snitch." T.A. admired their courage. They could have easily turned on him yet had not. He felt compelled to acknowledge their realness and express his gratitude for that quality.

"Don't worry about that loser ass bum, the game's gonna serve her a cold dish on a rusty silver platter. I'm just thankful to have some live stand-up bitches in my corner. It's every niggas dream to wake-up and be able to live the way I do, and hoes all around the globe would die to have the nuts that it took for y'all to flip that pussy ass special prosecutor the middle finger."

"Baby, you know I got your back one hundred and ten percent. I knew what I was getting myself into when I started fucking with you T., so therefore however this shit turns out we gone go through it together, and I pledge that to you on my soul."

"That's some real shit - in life a person has to live by principles, principles that they'll be willing to lay their life down for if need be. Something most of these lames seem to have missed in game school. But we gone show 'em that ain't nothing sexier than a happy hoe wit' a tight lip," he said while pulling them both toward him on the oversized divan.

Chapter Eighteen

The vicinity near Estabrook Park was free of passersby, and as always traffic was next to none at this time of morning. Even in the daytime, the diminutive park, located on the upper east side of town, housed minimal activity compared to most recreational areas within the city, making it the perfect setting for anyone aiming at invisibility. Thus, the reason Agent Daley elected to meet with Li Chan there at three in the morning. After calling her with the time and place, he began driving around all sides of the park's perimeter in a shady grey Pontiac Grand Prix, that no one except his younger brother Shane knew existed.

Chan showed up on schedule to the designated spot a few minutes early and phoned her blackmailer at 3am sharp confirming her arrival.

"I'm here, where are you?" she said getting straight to the point.

"I'll be there in a second agent relax," he said pretending as if he hadn't already spotted her knowing precisely where Chan was.

"Okay, how much longer, I thought you would be prompt," she said looking around. Li understood how the F.B.I. worked and wasn't taking the situation for granted. Sure she figured he was on the up and up, but one could never be too certain they had all sorts of tricks.

"Relax, relax I'm coming, I'll see you shortly," he said then hung up before she could come with another response. He too was paranoid, on his way to their little meeting Daley thought over a double cross, after applying the squeeze to someone careful calculations would tell anyone that underestimating your mark was equivalent to suicide.

After he watched for another minute or so, Daley put away his night vision binoculars inside the glove compartment and set off to attain his prize.

As he pulled in off the road, Chan sat patiently at a bench near a brown Milwaukee County Park System sign that read "Estabrook Park Area 3." She showed no fear as her once loyal partner exited the vehicle and approached.

"You know Li; I must say that I'm not at all surprised by you actually showing up. You've always been witty when it came to reason," he said taking a seat next to her. "But I'm not so sure about this thing with you and the pimp. We've got his black ass in a sling, and there's nothing you or anyone else can do about it," he said referring to Keyshawn.

"Too bad you won't be getting the Meritorious Achievement Award," she said speaking of a medal that the FBI issued for extraordinary and exceptional service during an investigation.

"Very funny, I see you've developed a sense of humor, which is good because I hear being a single mom can be a bit of a pain in the ass at times," he said shooting back.

"I'm sure it couldn't be any worse than having no life outside of work agent." This ticked him off somewhat.

"Okay enough of the funny shit, where's my money?" he said glancing at medium sized Tote bag Chan had sitting on the ground alongside of her.

"Here's your money, but before I give it to you I need to have your assurance that you'll stick to your word and won't try any funny business after this," she said placing the bag in her lap.

"The only way you'll know that is by me giving you my word, which I'm sure, means nothing to you by now. However, I hold the remote to this show and therefore just sit back and watch. Now give me my fucking money," he said snatching the bag aggressively. Understanding that whatever she had said at this point would mean nothing to him, Chan allowed him to maintain the floor.

"I'm sure it's all here, but in the event that it isn't our agreement here tonight is null and void," he said preparing to turn and walk away.

Again Chan didn't respond, instead she rose and turned left heading in the opposite direction.

As he moved along toward his vehicle Daley was elated that his scheme had actually panned out, but that lasted only briefly as overconfidence over his wit began to take its course. He then centered his attention on what he would do with the money.

"Fifty-thousand dollars seems sufficient for the amount of work I put in to nail their asses. And to think she actually believes I'm gonna honor that bullshit agreement," he said to himself just seconds from stepping onto the pavement where his car was parked.

But before he could place another foot on the soil his stride was interrupted by two bullets to the back. As he fell Daley turned to see Chan advancing towards him unscrewing the silencer from the black Sig 226 9mm. At the same time a navy blue utility van arrived carrying four men, all clothed in dark colors.

"Good timing fellas," Chan said reaching for the moneybag on the ground.

"Toss me the burner," Tiahmo responded referring to the murder weapon, as the other three bounded Daley's hands and feet before taping up his mouth and hauling him over to the van. The entire task took under a minute, and all parties had vanished in two.

Chapter Nineteen

By 4 a.m., the crowd at Potawatomi Casino had thinned down to well under a few hundred. With the exception of the regular gamblers and late night hustlers, the only people who remained were the casino hypes bouncing from table to table in hopes of eventually hitting that big lick or the one's who'd already lost days prior but were still roaming the floor searching for a fresh face to solicit ten or twenty dollars from for a another round of spins at a slot machine.

Paris had been lingering around black jack tables near the high rollers section for the past hour hoping to score a last minute trick. She'd broke luck earlier that night for a mere two hundred but wasn't satisfied with the take and decided to score one more before calling it a night. As she strolled along an isle leading to the restroom area her prayers were answered.

"Excuse me Miss, may I have a second of your time please?" a voice said from her rear. Before entering the women's room, she turned to assess the action. Being young, tall, clean cut, and Caucasian he met all of her requirements. In the past Paris could have cared less about his makeup, as long as he was looking to spend money any of that wouldn't have mattered. But the rape incident she encountered with the Mexican had taught her a valuable lesson in the phrase of "all money not being good money." Since then Paris learned to choose her clients and a small 25-caliber handgun now accompanied her on all dates.

"Sure you can, as long as you don't waste it," she responded with a pleasant schoolgirl smile. He laughed it off.

"Okay, in that case let me get right to the point. I think you're absolutely beautiful and I'd like to get to know you, so how about you have breakfast with me this morning?" he said with a sly grin.

"I don't know that depends on where and for how long, my time is valuable," she said setting the stage.

"My condo and for however long you'd like."

"I'm sure, but again my time is valuable," she said one last time.

"I understand is the meter running yet?"

"It sure is, it started running as soon as you stopped me," she said as they both shared a brief chuckle.

"Well shall we proceed to our destination then?"

"I don't see why not," she responded.

The walk to the exit was brief and as the valet person returned in the black seven series, BMW Paris re-contemplated total costs and fees. "In this game more wealth renders a greater fee" she remembered a quote Venus would say anytime they would come upon rich clients.

When the climbed inside the beamer before pulling off, he produced his wallet and slid her five hundred dollar bills.

"I figure that should be a sufficient enough down payment," he said halfway posing it as a question.

"It's fine, thank you Mr. Mystery man whose name I don't even know."

"Excuse my manners, I'm Brad and you are?"

"Nice to meet you Brad, I'm Paris," they both giggled as he hit the accelerator heading out of the parking lot.

Paris was ecstatic, but knew better than to reveal her hand; it had been a long time since she had serviced a high-end client. Every since Key banished her from his stable it was as if she'd lost her Mo-Jo, but that was yesterday and today would be a new beginning. Cursing along Canal Street Paris made a vow to herself that from now on she would go harder than she had ever done! "I don't need him or no other pimp for that matter; I got the game to do whatever I choose to on my own." She somewhat felt like herself again.

~ ❖ ~

All six windows on the Ford Escort were beginning to fog up as they went at it in the backseat. Driven deep off in a wooded area just three minutes north of the city, the two eighteen years old were comfortable as could be in their favorite late-night rendezvous spot.

"You're not gonna leave your pants on this time are you Jess?" the young boy said licking on the left side of her neck and ear.

"Toby you know I don't like taking them all the way off, I mean what if someone walks up on us," she said as her eyes rolls about from the arousal.

"Oh come on, no one's coming out here this late and you know it. As many times, as we've been here you should know that by now. Just pull them off this time for me will ya?" he said in a pleading voice.

"Okay." He stroked her long blonde curls while kissing her all over the face she began to remove her trousers. As always, the glimpse of her silky matching pubic hair nearly drove him to ecstasy before they could get started. Before she could utter another word, he was down to his boxers exposing an erection.

"Come here," he said lying on top while pulling her close until their bodies met. Feeling electrified, she purred as he widened her legs and entered gently.

They began to rock rhythmically to the pace of a love song in the CD player.

"Oh baby I love you," she said holding his face attempting to look into his eyes. Then suddenly a light appeared to be moving towards them.

"Toby, somebody's out there." She said looking up over his shoulders.

"Huh what, "he said concentrating on reaching a climax.

"I said somebody's coming now, look." The light had gotten close enough now that she was able to make out the object before them. Glancing up momentarily, he could see the figure as well it was a van.

"Don't worry about that, it's nothing," he said taking deep strokes.

"No, I'm not comfortable, get up."

"Oh Jess...."

"Look, they're getting out, they're getting out!" she said cutting him off. Completely turned off by now, he rolled off her to focus on their visitors. Jess was hastily retrieving her garments and placing them back on.

The two men who had emerged from the driver and passenger doors of the utility van were headed to the rear of the vehicle. Once there, they opened up the swinging doors and Tiahmo climbed out handing them flashlights and shovels as they began conversing.

"Turn the radio down they might hear it," Jess said whispering. Although there was no way for them to be heard, they were at least a hundred yards apart with the lights out and so many trees surrounding them that the only real way for them to be discovered was by the men closing in on their immediate area.

"Relax, they can't hear us," Toby said hoping that he was right.

The two men with shovels walked a few feet away from where the van was parked and laid everything in their hands down then returned to the van. Just as they made it, Tiahmo was reaching back inside and began to pull out the bag containing Agent Daley's body.

"You mind pushing a little harder up there? This muthafucka' ain't all that light ya' know" he was saying to the fourth member of the crew who wasn't as big and strong as the rest of them.

"I'm pushing damn" the man shot back.

"Somebody jump up in there and help this dude please, I'm not trying to be out here all night fucking with this shit." As one of the joined up top, the other assisted Tiahmo on his end.

"Oh my God Toby, I hope they're not carrying what I think they are in the bag baby," she said feeling nervous now.

"Shhhh, be quiet," he said attempting to make out what they were saying.

After hauling the body over to a hole they had dug the previous night, two of them grabbed the shovels while the others provided them with light to finish the job.

"Them fucking feds gonna be everywhere looking for his ass by tomorrow, but it'll surely be in vain," Tiahmo said laughing. The others didn't say a word instead they continued filling up the hole they'd dumped him in with dirt.

Jess was petrified even Toby had become a little shaken; they grew up in an affluent neighborhood where scary looking guys walking through the woods with dead bodies were things you only seen in the movies.

"Oh my God, oh my God, Toby we have to do something," she said.

"Shhh shut-up! There is nothing we can do that persons already dead. Just be calm until they leave, otherwise I'm sure they kill us too," he said out of pure fear.

"I'm scared," she said in a trembling voice.

"I know, like I said just relax they don't know we're here so we'll be fine."

Once the hole was fully covered, they packed it down before locating some sticks and leaves to add over the top of the grave for extra insurance, then made their way back to the van and commenced to heading in the path of the two onlookers.

Startled the only thing they could think of was to sink down into the seat as far as possible to avoid detection. Hearing the engine approaching Jess clutched her boyfriend's arm with what seemed like was the strength of Sylvester Stallone in the peak of his bodybuilding days. But good fortune was on their sides that night, the driver turned onto a path about thirty yards to the left of them.

When Toby heard him changing course he raised his head up in an attempt to get a make on the van, and immediately spotted its plate number. Then as soon as the vans rear light were out of their frightened sights the pair didn't waste any time springing into action.

"It's time to get the hell out of here," Toby said cranking up the engine and heading out in the opposite direction.

"I'm calling the police," the girl said while dialing 911.

~ ❖ ~

She swayed back and forth barely conscious Paris was pushing herself to stay awake. But the mickey that he'd placed in her vodka was far too strong for anyone to overcome its spell.

"How's the drink baby?" Brad said while caressing her hair. He was all work no play soon as they had reached the condo Paris had made the foolish mistake of allowing him to prepare their drinks as she'd freshened up in his bathroom. She was nearly non-responsive.

"I see it worked out fine" Brad, whose real name was "Santino," was hired by Keyshawn to disable Paris before any indictment or trial took place. It was Chan's position that she needed to be permanently impaired mentally, an idea that Keyshawn concurred. They didn't want bodies popping up everywhere for fear of being discovered by the bureau. So instead, they decided that stealing her memory and sanity would be just as effective.

Paris was trying to speak, but her mind was in a state of utter confusion. The only thing the drugs allowed her to do was move her limbs at an extremely slow pace. She had played her last hand as a prostitute from here on out life as she knew it would never be the same. The dose that he had administered would surely keep her brain at a complete scatter for the next decade of two at a minimum. Paris believed that she could navigate her way through the game successfully alone; again, her calculations had been incorrect.

The mind assassin dialed his contact person as he sat next to her paying close attention to her pulse. A few times he had added too much of a dosage, causing the victims to expire.

"It's done bring the remaining balance along with my ticket. And be here no later than 7am sharp," he said before hanging up the call. They had had him flown in two days prior from Cincinnati, leaving the condo once to bait his mark at the casino and the next time he'd tour Milwaukee would be on his way to the airport.

At 6:30 am sharp the door came down, it sounded as if a shotgun had gone off in the next room, knowing who it was Keyshawn didn't move. Instead, he sat up at the edge of his bed and waited for them to make their way up the stairs and bum rush his room. They heavily armed agents and Marshals were there in seconds.

"Lay on the bed face down Keyshawn," said the first agent that entered the room. He did as he was told.

"We have a federal warrant for your arrest," said another one as Chan came strolling in the room. They both looked at one another; he wasn't worried about the timing. Chan had already informed him about the bureau's policy about executing potentially violent detainees. The higher-ups never informed field agents on exactly when it would take place. When they arrived at the office, the teamed would be quickly assembled and briefed before action.

After reading him his Miranda rights a huge Caucasian Marshal escorted him through the living area where the girls were all sitting on the floor wearing zip ties, ready to be taken into custody.

"Every game has an end Watson," one of them said as he was passing on the way out the door.

"Fuck you fag," he said walking through the threshold.

~ ❖ ~

At the same time T.A. was being nabbed by Agents Collins and another team; when they hit his door the gym buff was in his kitchen watching the early morning news.

"Can I at least finish my meal, I heard they have terrible food service down there where you guys work," he said while sitting at the table eating a piece of grapefruit. They granted his request, and then hauled him off without hesitation.

Chapter Twenty

When the Brown Deer Police Department responded to the 911 call, they discovered Daley's body just where she said it was. And as they began taping off the crime scene two officers brought the two teens back to the area in hopes that they could provide descriptive details as to what actually took place earlier that morning. With the officers surrounding them, they were at ease and felt safe speaking to investigator after investigator.

A crime of this magnitude was unheard of in this region of the state. So naturally, word had spread throughout the county in no time. Soon after, several outlets of media had surface to cover the story. From television news channels to radio stations by 7:30am the landscape was swarming with reporters.

Entering the building, she immediately understood that Daley's death and identity were made known; several agents were slumped over in chairs morning the esteemed agent. She went straight to Benders office. Morgan was there with him arranging an itinerary as he prepared to go on-site at the scene of the crime.

"Jesus sir, I'm hearing that they....," Chan said pretending as she walked through the door. Bender appeared to be at a loss for words as he turned to look back from the window. He spoke slowly and deliberately.

"Yes, we've lost a fine young man agent," Bender said cutting her off.

"But sir what happened to him?" she said trying to obtain all the information she could.

"Well now that we're not too sure of the only thing that we do know at this point is that he was taken there by a group of black males in some sort of blue van. Hearing that made her heart dropped.

"That's odd," she said waiting for more information to flow from him.

"Tell me about it I'm leaving now to find out more first hand, they have two teens that seem to have witnessed it all and they claim to have physical descriptions of the suspects. We are waiting on Madison to give us the green light to take over the investigation. I'm sure that by now that hick department probably screwed up the entire area," he said heading for the door.

"Let's hope not, I can't believe this, not Daley," Chan expressed partly hurt.

"I know, but now we must do our best of finding out who did this to him and bring them to their fucking knees. What animal would do a thing like this?"

Bender was furious over Daley's murder and was willing to do whatever it took at getting to the very bottom of it.

"We have every available branch of this office working on this one and I won't stop until these dirt bags are in the death chamber in Indiana!" The state of Wisconsin itself didn't have the death penalty, but killing a federal agent in any state could be punishable by death considering the circumstances of the crime, especially if the agent was on duty.

"Sir, what would you like me to do?" Chan said sadly.

"Not to worry agent, we're on it. Finish the things you're already working on. I hear the apprehension of Watson and Smith went well, that's good. We can't let these bastards out here get away with anything!" he said angrily. Chan didn't respond.

"Please excuse my language agent, it's just very sickening to me," he said looking at her with weary eyes.

"It's okay sir, I understand, we lost a part of our team today I know how you feel," she said speaking from the heart. Chan was genuinely troubled by her partner's murder, but in her mind, it was something that had to be done. She gazed about aimlessly for a brief moment before excusing herself from the office to find out more.

~ ❖ ~

When S.A.I.C. Bender left his office, Morgan approached him.

"Sir, the conference room is ready for the briefing," she said speaking rapidly.

"Conference room, for what?" he was lost for a moment.

"With the media sir."

"Oh, yes of course. Let's make this quick," he said with a sigh. As they entered the room, he could smell the adrenaline seeping from the pores of the correspondents all eager to be the first at break any imperative news regarding the morning's events. He wasn't even given a chance to reach the podium before cameras began rolling and the clicking of Kodak's apprehended the silence. But all was quiet as he began.

"Yesterday the government was able to secure indictments on two of the most violent and vicious prostitution rings that this country has ever seen. T.A. Smith and Keyshawn Watson were named in a four count indictment as heads of both these rings," he said pointing to mug shots of them that had been blown-up into posters.

"These individuals were in total control of both the outfits mentioned, and the F.BI. believes that this city is safer with them now being in custody. We have seized realty property, luxury automobiles, and several pieces of high-end jewelry; some valued as much as fourth thousand dollars. We are confident that the government will prevail in these cases and that all parties involved will be dealt the necessary consequences for their action. At this time we'll have a few questions." The room instantly seemed like an auction house as Bender started answering the journalists' questions.

"Agent, what are the charges that their being held on?" a stubby bald reporter said while scribbling something down onto a miniature notepad.

"The charges range from crimes of Interstate Trafficking of Prostitutes to Bribery of a Public Official," Bender said quickly before moving on to the next question.

"Agent, can you please tell us the connection between the people you named here and Alderman Billings?" a tall woman wearing a pinstriped jacket said.

"Alderman Jonathan Billings will indeed face charges for crimes involving him that we have uncovered."

"What can you tell us about the investigation into the death of agent Greg Daley?" said a one of the younger writers.

"That's all the time we have, thanks for the questions folks," Bender said before rushing away from the stand.

~ ❖ ~

In a cell at the bureau's field investigations headquarters Collins began to conduct the interrogation of Keyshawn. He was banking on his ace in the hole (Chan) to push into debriefing. The first thing he did was shoved pictures of her on the table as he sparked the conversation.

"Nice looking woman you have there huh," he said as if it was a question. Keyshawn didn't respond nor react to the pictures.

"Oh I see you're a hard ass, well what if I told you that your pretty little Asian whom you thought was a hooker is actually one of our agents?" a pause.

"Then I'd still tell you the same thing, talk to my lawyer." And just like that the interrogation was over with.

~ ❖ ~

In route to the Brown Deer Bender's team went over intelligence and strategy.

"Have we found anything on the owner of that van?" he said taking a Tylenol.

"Yes, it turned up registered to a female, black, age 23, name Janay Henderson."

"Good, have we made contact with her yet?" Bender said cutting him off.

"Two agents went by her place about a half hour ago. Henderson claims that the van does belong to her. She says that her ex-boyfriend whom she shares a child with actually owns the vehicle and that he paid her to put the van in her name eight months ago."

"Okay, makes sense, so what do we know about this guy?" Bender said attempting to block the headache out of his mind.

"Name's Tiahmo Lewis, has a very extensive and violent arrest record, currently serving a two year probation sentence for a gun charge," said agent Ramirez.

"So where are we with him?" Bender said studying his photo.

"I spoke with his probation agent's supervisor during your news conference. Turns out he has a home visit scheduled for today between the hours of 7am and noon." Bender glanced at his watch it was 10:30.

"Who does he live with? And do we have the cooperation of D.O.C. on this?"

"He's on file with the Department of Correction as living with his mother; however through investigations we have indeed learned this isn't actually his residence, and yes they're willing to work with us on bringing him in. A perimeter has been put in place and his agent is currently on stand-by with our people," he said in with confidence.

"Alright, I want to be there when this thing goes down, have this truck re-routed and send someone else to cover the crime scene" Bender said. Ramirez went into action immediately, Bender always enjoyed working with him, and he was extremely thorough and possessed a profound ability to think on his feet.

T.A. wondered how much his bail would be, he had nearly a half of a million cash stashed away. Not including income properties that he shared with his dad. All things that the government didn't have access to, the only thing that bore in his name was the club and based on the bribery charges he was pretty sure the feds would try their best to seize it. But it wasn't a lost that he couldn't afford.

"It was a good thing that bitch pulled our coats to shit when she did, otherwise we'd really be screwed," he said aloud to himself in relief. Just then, the door opened.

"Hello Mr. Smith, I'm agent Collins, you mind if we talk for a few minutes?"

"Talk about what homie?" T.A. said with a frown.

"You guys are in a lot of trouble, we have wire-taps, witnesses, and a list of other things that you have working against you my friend." Collins had just left the room where another agent was handling the interrogation of Alderman Billings; he began debriefing long before he had even made it downtown. With what he had confirmed along with additional information, they were able to gather Collins grew even more confident that a conviction was under-way in the near future.

"You basically have two choices here my man, either tell us all that you know or go away for the remainder of your youth? So what'll it be?" he said leaning forward on his palms starring at T.A.

"When do I see a judge?" was his response.

"The last thing you need to be worried about is seeing a judge brother. Right now, you need to be focused on helping yourself and us so that when you do see a judge he might, that's right I said might! Have some compassion for you." Collins said sarcastically. T.A. took a long hard look at Collins.

"Get outta' here man, I don't wanna here this bullshit. Y'all do what y'all have to and me and my lawyers, yeah muthafucka' I said lawyers! We'll do the same," he said giving the agent a wicked glance. "Now if you don't mind I have some thinking to do," he said before leaning back on the steal seat and looking away.

Chapter Twenty-One

At 11:10 am, Chan arrived, dressed down in tennis shoes and jeans, with a blue FBI jacket and body armor. After hearing word that they were moving in on Tiahmo, she rushed over to their location to monitor the outcome.

"Chan you didn't have to come we have it covered," Bender said as she climbed in the back of the Suburban.

"I know sir, but I owe it to Greg," she said acting.

"Okay well, the probation guy will walk to the door with one of our people who are undercover posing as a cover agent for the D.O.C. We will not move in until our guy brandishes his weapon and has the suspect at bay. At which time unit one will..."

"Sir, everyone's ready," agent Ramirez, said.

"Okay, Chan you understand the play. Remember people I want this guy taking in unharmed if possible, he didn't act alone, and we need him to lead us to his friends," Bender said before Ramirez began speaking again.

"Sir, they are approaching the house."

~ ❖ ~

He was home alone cooking pancakes and sausage for himself when the door rang.

"It's about time this slow ass muthafucka' made it here," he said placing the spatula on the stove. As he was walking to the Tiahmo stopped to peak out of the blinds, a habit he would develop that was strictly out of paranoia. He wasn't at all alarmed by seeing someone with his probation officer; after all it wasn't the first time.

The interior door had a deadbolt lock along with an additional one on the doorknob. After unlatching both, he opened it and began on the security gate. In the process of turning the lock, Tiahmo noticed the shadow of an agent standing still on left side of the home near the front. His mind instantaneously went to the murder they had committed just hours ago. He jumped back, slammed the door, and ran to retrieve his weapon from the kitchen cabinet.

Both men at the entrance turned and ran towards a car filled with agents who were now exiting with guns drawn.

"Move away from the house and stand down," Bender screamed over the radio. As everyone scrambled to find positioning; at a safe distance away from the dwelling; the tactical unit swarmed the entire area. Dozens of federal agents equipped with armored helmets, shields, and high-powered AR-15 assault rifles were now situated in various spots along front and rear of the house; as snipers planted themselves - aiming steadily as they waited for their next order.

When the massive mobile command pulled up at the corner of the block Tiahmo was on the second floor peeking out of a bedroom window located at the front of the house. Not willing to concede, he looked around as carefully as he could to find any viable escape route, there was none.

"SHIT!!," he said aloud as he sat with his back up against the wall clutching the hundred round Mac-11 thinking of a way out.

Looking outside again the young solider thought, he had seen a familiar face, and at a second glance, he realized that he had. It was Chan; better known to him as "Key's bitch Kimmie." He had only seen her twice in life; once during planning and then at the execution, but she had features that were unmistakable to him. Not to mention the fact that he had seen her just hours earlier.

"What the FUCK? That bitch is a Fed., he said looking at her attire." He was confused, if Kimmie was a Fed. did that mean they'd set him up? His thoughts were racing now. Tiahmo never knew Kimmie's true identity. Keyshawn and T.A. didn't feel it necessary to expose that to him, they both agreed that the less he and anybody else knew about that the better. Nor had either one of them anticipated their plan going this far south.

"This is the F.B.I., Tiahmo Lewis you have five minutes to come out of the house with your hands up or we will have no choice but to enter the home with force," Bender said yelling from a bullhorn.

As Bender was speaking, Chan visualized his surrender. "What if they crack him and he rolls on everyone?" This was not just any murder, a federal agent was dead, and she knew that the bureau would do whatever it took to find out why and exactly by whose hand. Even if it meant letting the actually trigger man walk away with a lighter sentence than the orchestrators.

"They gotta' be fucking crazy thinking I'm coming out there," he said to himself. Then suddenly he began to think of the possibilities and various outcomes of not adhering to their demands. None were pleasant, but all sounded better than what they had in store for him had he complied.

"This punk ass bitch, she set me up I know it. I'm gone waste this hoe before these pussies take me out," he said looking out the window seeking a clear visual of her. Tiahmo fixed his mind on dying, but it wouldn't be alone.

To be continued . . .

To learn more about Swift visit:

www.swiftnovels.com

ORDER FORM

Motivation
Book Series

-BARGAINS RATES -
PURCHASE ANY 2 BOOKS FOR ONLY $20.00
PURCHASE THE ENTIRE MOTIVATION BOOK
SERIES FOR ONLY $28.00!!

Quantity	Book Title	Cost	Total
	MOTIVATION MASTERING THE GAME	$11.99	
	MOTIVATION II THE CHASE	$12.99	
	MOTIVATION III THE EXIT	$14.99	
	VIA U.S. PRIORITY MAIL S/H $2.99 FIRST BOOK $1.00 EA ADDITIONAL BOOK WISCONSIN RESIDENTS MUST ADD 5.6% SALES TAX		
	Total Submitted		

MAKE CHECK & MONEY ORDERS PAYABLE TO:
R.H. PUBLISHING, LLC P.O. BOX 11642 MILWAUKEE, WI 53211

Name_____

ID#_____

Institution Name_____

Address_____

City_____ State _____ Zip _____

FOR ONLINE ORDERS VISIT:
www.swiftnovels.com

Made in the USA
Coppell, TX
12 October 2020

39664465R00115